THREADS of *Destiny*
TAPESTRIES

N.J. WALTERS

ELLORA'S CAVE
ROMANTICA®
www.EllorasCave.com

An Ellora's Cave Publication

www.ellorascave.com

Threads of Destiny

ISBN 9781419963940
ALL RIGHTS RESERVED.
Threads of Destiny Copyright © 2009 N.J. Walters
Edited by Pamela Campbell.
Cover art by Syneca.

Electronic book publication January 2009
Trade paperback publication 2011

THREADS OF DESTINY

ဆ

Dedication

෴

This book is for everyone who fell in love with the Tapestries series, especially with Marc Garen. I've never had so many emails about one particular character. So for all of you who wrote demanding – I mean asking for – Marc's story, this one is for you.

As always, thank you to my amazingly supportive husband.

Chapter One

ℰℐ

A hard, muscled arm wrapped around her waist, making her gasp. Before she could react, Kathryn Piedmont was dragged up against a solid male chest. "You're late," a rough, masculine voice whispered in her ear.

She relaxed as soon as he spoke, recognizing the voice. "I couldn't get away any sooner. I have to act as normal as possible, especially now."

Tienan's arm loosened and she stepped away from him. Reaching out, she hit the light switch on the wall by the entrance, illuminating the suite of rooms that she occupied in her family's palatial home. As always, the room seemed to press in on her with its drab colors and dark furniture. Sighing, she rubbed her temples.

"Hard day?" She managed to smile at the other man lounging on an antique settee in the corner. About six-foot-two with wide shoulders, he looked even more masculine in contrast to the fragile piece of furniture. His short blond hair was standing up in spikes on top of his head, reminding her of his habit of dragging his fingers through it when he was agitated. Still, from looking at him, you wouldn't know he had a care in the world.

"It wasn't easy." She softened her tone and tried to send him a reassuring smile. Though he didn't show it outwardly, Kathryn knew that Logan was the more sensitive of the two. She knew just how much trouble both these men were in. How much trouble she would be in if her father found them in her rooms.

Tienan grunted and began prowling around the room and she knew he was thinking, calculating their options and their chances of success. But that wasn't unusual. He was always thinking. He had a computer-like brain that never stopped. Both men had off-the-chart IQs but Tienan was able to remove emotion from the equation. It was his greatest strength and consequently, his greatest weakness.

Tienan was the same height as Logan but that's where the similarity ended. Where Logan's hair was blond and short, Tienan's fell to his shoulders in a straight black curtain. His body was leaner but no less muscular. He reminded her of a jaguar she'd seen in an old film—all coiled muscles, just waiting to attack. Both men were handsome. Tienan was good-looking in a classic sense, while Logan possessed more of a craggy, rough look that was impossible to ignore.

They were also her friends and, as of yesterday, her responsibility.

"What's the word on the jail break?" Logan sat forward, his hands loosely clasped between his legs.

Kathryn strode across the room, trying to appear confident as she dumped her sweater and purse on a chair. Her stomach burned from all the stress of the day and she rubbed her hand across it, trying to settle it. She knew she had the beginnings of an ulcer. The doctor had warned her at her last appointment that she needed to take better care of herself. Easier said than done.

Tienan's green eyes narrowed and he stalked to the mini-fridge that was tucked into a cabinet in the corner. Opening the door, he pulled out a small container of milk. He unscrewed the top as he strode to her side. "Drink."

Grateful for the slight reprieve, she took the plastic bottle, brought it to her lips and drank. The cool liquid coated her throat and hit her stomach like a cooling balm. Sighing with relief, she licked her lips. "Thanks."

One corner of Tienan's mouth turned up in a slight smile as he reached out and used his thumb to wipe away a bead of milk from the corner of her mouth. Bringing it to his lips, he licked it away. "My pleasure."

She could see the barely banked heat in his eyes and it set her blood racing. The corner of her mouth tingled where he'd touched her and her stomach fluttered again. This time it had nothing to do with her burgeoning ulcer.

Neither Tienan nor Logan were being shy about the fact that they wanted her. She was very attracted to both of them as well, had been for years. She'd never acted on that attraction and neither had they. They knew that to do so would bring serious consequences for them all. Kathryn shivered at the thought of what her father might do if he ever discovered how much both men meant to her. Certainly, she'd never see them again. And that was probably the least of it.

There was no doubt they were both handsome men but it was more than that. Kathryn knew them to be good men, honorable man, unlike her father and the General. But there was no place in her life to indulge in an affair — with either of them. All their lives were in danger.

"Tienan." There was a warning note in Logan's voice, telling him to back off. The tension between the three of them was mounting with every moment they spent together in close confines.

Tienan glanced at his friend and then back at her, his expression blank. "Tell us what happened."

Carrying her container of milk with her, Kathryn made her way to one of the velvet wingback chairs and sank down into it as exhaustion swamped her. "You'd think that in this advanced year of 2133 this kind of thing wouldn't happen." She was living it. Heck, she was part of it but that didn't mean she understood it.

"Kathryn." Logan's softer voice pulled her back to the task at hand. He rose from the settee and came over to kneel by her feet, taking her hand in his much larger one. "Tell us."

His brows were furrowed and she could see the concern in his eyes.

"The security breach was discovered just after we left last night." Beads of sweat formed on her forehead as she thought about how close they'd come to being discovered. "They've been questioning—" she broke off and gave a shaky laugh. "No, they were *interrogating* everyone all day. They think your release must have been facilitated by one of the terrorist factions from outside the Gate."

The Gate, as it was referred to, was really a high-tech shield, which protected the enclosed city from contamination from the outside. Climate-controlled and almost impenetrable, the ruling class lived inside the safe urban confines, while everyone else resided outside in poverty, filth and disease.

Her family, the Piedmonts, was part of the upper crust. In fact, her father was a member of the Ruling Council. Her ancestors had lived in this mansion for more than one hundred fifty years, amassing wealth and power. When the wars, natural disasters and disease had struck after 2015, her family had risen even higher, being major players in such things as hydroponics, genetic research, pharmaceuticals, oil and weapons. When the dust had settled, what remained of the world had been segregated into two distinct classes—those who ruled and everybody else.

Tienan gave a grunt of satisfaction. "Their misdirection should give us a few days to figure out what to do while they run around chasing their own tails." His disdain of the security force was well known.

"I'm not so sure." Kathryn set her milk container aside and rubbed her forehead. She had a massive headache brewing. "General Caruthers is not convinced."

Both men froze at the mention of his name. Known for his brutal ways and iron fist, the General, as he was called by one and all, was a man to be feared. Any resistance to the will of the Ruling Council, of which he was a member, was dealt with swiftly and without mercy. The man had spies everywhere and was in full control of the security forces. If there was one man to be feared, it was he.

It was the General who'd decided that Project Alpha had been a failure and that the test subjects needed to be terminated. Since Tienan and Logan were the test subjects in question, there was no love lost between them and the General.

Tienan growled low in his throat and, once again, Kathryn was reminded of a lethal animal just waiting to pounce and devour his prey. She shook her head and then had to stifle a groan as pain shot through her skull. "You should be safe here for another day or two. After that…" she trailed off, not wanting to consider what might happen if they didn't find a way to get both men out of the city.

"Are you in any immediate danger?" Logan gently squeezed her fingers.

"I don't think so." She refused to tell them just how terrifying the interrogation had been for her. The General himself had questioned her for hours. She had bruises on her upper arms where he'd dragged her out of her chair and shoved her against the wall. His breath had been hot against her skin as he'd spewed his venomous anger. He all but accused her of helping the men escape. Only his knowledge of whom her father was had saved her from imprisonment or worse. But she knew that wouldn't save her for long. And if her father discovered what she'd done, he'd personally hand her over to the General.

"Kathryn?" Tienan came to crouch beside her.

"I don't know, okay?" She jumped to her feet, needing some space. "I need to think." She headed for the door. "Stay here and hide if anyone comes. They might do a random search for security reasons."

"We know where the tunnels are," Logan assured her.

That was the one good thing about living in this huge mausoleum that she called home. Her ancestors had built several escape routes and they'd used them more than once over the years. Now she was using them to hide her friends. She wasn't even sure her father knew they existed. She only knew because of some old blueprints she'd found in the attic.

"Kathryn," Logan began but she shook her head, not wanting to talk about the situation any longer. The memories of her traumatic day were still too fresh. She needed some time alone. It would be easy to lay her head on Logan's shoulder and cry and that she couldn't do. She had to be strong if they were to have a chance at surviving.

The attic. That was what she needed right now. Space to think. "I'll be back in a bit." Not giving them a chance to question her further, she hurried out the door, taking care to close it behind her. There was no one around as she made her way to a door at the end of the east wing of the house. It was late and most of the servants had departed. Her father disliked having too many people in his home and only a trusted few actually lived in the house. The rest lived in barracks on the estate. The security guards were stationed outside. They were a constant.

She looked around before she opened the door enough to squeeze through. She needed no light to find the stairs and climb them. She'd been coming to the attic for years, since she was a teenager. It was her private space. A place not tainted by her father's presence.

Opening the door at the top of the stairs, she sighed with relief as she stepped inside and flipped on the light. Years ago, she'd cleared out a corner, setting up an old comfortable chair and table for her own use. She went to that chair now and sank into its welcoming depths. What was she going to do?

Burying her face in her hands, she took a deep breath. Her father and his team of scientists had started Project Alpha about thirty years before. They'd gone beyond the Gate to find victims for the experiment.

Using a mixture of genetic engineering and computer programming, they'd created male babies who would grow into alphas. Their purpose was to be faster, stronger and to live much longer than any human. Their genetics were manipulated in such a way as to give them the best of everything. But they were also given computer implants to make learning quicker and to make them controllable by their handlers. The Ruling Council had decided that they needed an army of super-soldiers, men who would fight until they dropped and who were expendable. If Project Alpha were a success, they would use that technology to create a race of super-soldiers to protect them and the city against the ever-increasing unrest beyond the Gate.

Over the years, most of the subjects had been weeded out as unsuitable. Kathryn remembered how horrified she'd been by this when she'd come across the dusty old file several months ago. Many of the boys had barely reached ten years of age before they were murdered. She knew the scientists saw it as simply destroying expendable test subjects. To her it was outright genocide.

Now thirty years and many failed experiments later, they were ready to terminate this project. They'd been working on robotic soldiers for more than a decade now and these were deemed more acceptable to the task at hand.

There had been problems with Project Alpha.

The two remaining subjects had developed as they'd hoped, quickly becoming experts in martial arts and hand-to-hand combat as they grew. By the time they were twenty, they were experts in every weapon known to mankind. Unfortunately, rather than living longer, they were aging at a rate just the tiniest bit faster than humans. Their life expectancy was just around sixty to sixty-five years. Kathryn speculated that this was due to the extreme physical and emotional strain that they'd been under since the day they were born.

The scientists had also not counted on the men thinking for themselves. Even with the computer implants, they were not easy to control. They reasoned and thought and made their own decisions, plus they'd showed emotions, something the scientists had tried to breed and train out of them.

The Council deemed the experiment a complete failure and General Caruthers had ordered the termination of the two remaining Alphas—Alpha One and Alpha Two—Tienan and Logan.

Kathryn sat back, leaning her head against the cushions. She'd been the only one to object, the only one to find the edict heinous and unacceptable. The other scientists on the team had looked at her with pity and disdain as she reiterated the fact that Tienan and Logan were men, not machines. They were living, breathing people. No one listened. No one else cared.

A child prodigy, Kathryn was used to being viewed as unusual, as a freak of nature. She'd always been different, advancing quickly in her studies when she was young. Speed-reading was a talent that had allowed her to get through school quickly, that and a photographic memory. By the time she was twenty, she had advanced degrees in robotics, genetics and computer science, as well as degrees in botany and chemistry. By the time she was twenty-three, she'd added a medical degree to the list. Her father had supervised all her studies, pushing her harder as each year went by. Failure was not an option for a Piedmont. She had no friends and no life beyond her work. Kathryn had long felt like just another study subject, one who often disappointed.

For years, she had desperately wanted to leave this house and have a place of her own, a life of her own. But she was just as much a prisoner as Tienan and Logan. Rental units were at a premium inside the Gate. They were costly and offered only to those who met stringent requirements. Kathryn certainly had the pedigree to get one, but the one time she'd tried, her father had sent a note to the rental company and that had been that. The offer of the unit had been withdrawn, leaving her with nowhere else to go.

Her father often said it was for her personal safety but she knew better. He'd invested a lot of money in her over the years and Smithson Piedmont always made sure his investments paid off.

She'd gone to work at Piedmont Corporation at the ripe age of twenty-three and had begun working closely with Tienan and Logan. That was seven years, and seemed like a lifetime, ago. Back then, she'd believed in what she was doing. Back then she'd truly thought she could make a difference for good, to help the people beyond the Gate. It didn't take her long to discover that wasn't the objective of the Corporation. The only thing the Corporation cared about was making money and maintaining power.

The only good out of her time there was that she'd met Tienan and Logan. The same age as she, they'd become her friends.

Taking a deep breath, she reached out and plucked her favorite book from the table. Its cover now tattered and torn, she'd discovered it among a box of books in the far corner of the room a few months ago. She'd never read anything like those books in her life. They were filled with tales of erotic love and romance. For a woman who'd only had one single relationship in her life, which had been an unmitigated disaster, it had been a revelation.

Christina's Tapestry had quickly become her favorite of them all. The tale of a woman plucked from her mundane life and swept away to another place and time and into the arms of not one but two warriors had enthralled her. In the land of Javara, women were scarce and the brothers had engaged in a sexual competition in order to convince Christina to stay in their land and choose one of them as a husband. The men shared the woman but only one man could be her husband and claim the children as his own.

That was fine in a book, she supposed, but Kathryn didn't see how it could work in practice. It was fine for Christina and Jarek, the older brother in the book, but what about poor Marc? Although accepting of the arrangement, Marc had seemed lonely. As silly as it was, Kathryn had cried for Marc.

He was a special man and deserved a woman of his own. She'd actually gotten angry with the author for leaving him in such a state.

"Oh God," she moaned. "I'm losing my mind. I'm worried about a character in a book when Tienan and Logan's lives are in danger." She didn't want to think about what would happen to her if her part in this were ever discovered. Using their superior physical skills and intellect and her knowledge of the lab and the security systems at the various checkpoints in the city, they'd managed to get both men out of their confinement cells last night and away from Piedmont Corporation. Now, they had to figure out what to do next.

She wrapped her arms around herself, blinking back the tears that threatened. "What I need is a magical tapestry to whisk all three of us out of this mess." She smiled wistfully, thinking how nice it would be not to have to worry about her father, the General and the entire situation for just one day. Her entire life had been stressful for as far back as she could remember but the past few months that stress had increased tenfold. Exhaustion hit her and she knew she had to go back down to her rooms or eventually Tienan and Logan would come looking for her.

She pushed to her feet and stumbled slightly. She hadn't eaten since breakfast. The interrogation teams didn't concern themselves with such mundane things as food and water and now she was feeling lightheaded. Extending her hands to steady herself, she hit the corner of a small trunk. It slid off the top of the larger trunk it was resting on and crashed to the floor. "Shit!" She pitched forward, barely avoiding ending up face first on the floor.

The fallen trunk had popped open and she glanced inside as she wiped her hands on the legs of her pants and steadied herself. A leather-bound journal caught her eye and she plucked it from the depths of the trunk. It was obviously old, the leather cracked. Opening it carefully, she sucked in a breath when she realized it was from one of her ancestors, a woman who'd lived more than one hundred years before. "This is amazing." She turned one page, then another, reading rapidly.

Closing the book, she tucked it under her arm. She needed to read this. She was about to close the top of the trunk when something caught her eye. Plucking the bundle of fabric from the trunk, she shook it open, coughing and sneezing when dust flew from it. Carrying it closer to the light, she exclaimed with delight as the pattern emerged.

"Well, you wanted a tapestry." It was exactly as she imagined the one in the book would be and although it was dirty, she could see the myriad colors in the fabric. Red, green, blue, black, brown, white, silver and yellow all peeked from beneath the layer of dust, forming a picture. There was a stone castle in the center, surrounded by an abundance of flora and fauna, most of which she'd only seen in pictures. The river beyond the castle looked so real, she thought that if she touched it her fingers would get wet. "Incredible," she whispered. The colors would be positively vibrant after a good cleaning.

A man stood in front of the castle, tall and proud. He was dressed in brown pants and boots, his chest bare. Long brown hair fell to his waist and his golden-brown eyes seemed to stare at her, through her. Her nipples tightened dramatically, making her gasp. What was wrong with her? The longer she stared at him, the more aroused she became. Her panties were damp and her body felt heavy, almost lethargic.

This was crazy. It was definitely time to break out her vibrator. She groaned as she realized that wouldn't happen anytime soon. Not with Tienan and Logan staying with her. She'd spent the last seven years trying to think of them only as friends but with them here with her now that was becoming much more difficult. They were both handsome, virile men and she was only human after all. And she was a woman who, because of her commitment to her work and the lack of opportunity to meet someone who wasn't cowed by her father, hadn't had a man share her bed in over five years.

A noise startled her, sending her pulse racing. "Who's there?" She thought about what she'd heard. It had sounded almost as if someone had sighed. That was crazy. It was probably the wind in the eaves or something.

No one answered but she couldn't shake the feeling that she wasn't alone. She'd become very paranoid in the past few months, even more so in the past twenty-four hours. Draping the tapestry carefully over her chair, she laid the journal on top of it. She had to leave them here. She couldn't risk bringing them down to her room. If any of the staff discovered either item they'd tell her father and he'd have them thrown out just because they were important to her.

She closed the lid on the trunk and crept back to the door, listening carefully. After a few moments, her pounding heart settled and she cracked the door open. Seeing no one, she turned off the light and made her way down the stairs, placing each foot carefully on the step. A part of her wanted to bring the tapestry with her but logic prevailed.

"I wish that the tapestry was magic and it would bring Marc to me." She sighed, her words drifting back up the stairs, as she pulled open the door to the hallway. One night of hot sex with the man from her fantasies would at least relax her and maybe make it easier to face the coming days ahead. Her life was changing, no doubt about it. No matter what happened, she knew she couldn't stay here any longer. Tienan and Logan didn't know it yet but when they left the city, she was going with them.

Glancing up and down the hallway to make sure no one else was there, she sneaked back to her room, ready to face Tienan and Logan. They needed to make plans.

Chapter Two

❧

Marc Garen sat in his chair at the head table in the great hall, just beyond the feasting crowd, watching as friends, family and honored guests toasted the arrival of Jarek and Christina's third child. This one was cause for a major celebration. After two boys, they'd had a girl—a blonde-haired, blue-eyed beauty like her mother.

The child was the center of attention, her proud parents holding court as one person after another came to pay tribute. Their other two children, five-year-old Baron and three-year-old Derrik, stood beside them, looking proud and pleased. Even at their young age, they knew the importance of a female child.

Marc watched Baron, who smiled when he reached out and touched his sister's face with his chubby fingers. Although they'd both shared Christina's bed at the time, there was no doubt in Marc's mind that the boy was his. He felt it in his heart and soul but he could not claim him. Only Jarek, as Christina's husband, could claim the children as his own. It was the way things were done in Javara, the way they had to be done but that didn't make it any easier to accept.

Marc closed his eyes against the pain and emptiness that threatened to engulf him. He knew that both Jarek and Christina were worried about him. He'd shared their bed in the early days of their marriage, claiming his one night a week, as was his right as Jarek's brother. But in the past few years, those times had gotten farther and farther apart. It had been almost a year since he'd sought them out. They were so happy together that he always felt as if he were intruding.

Jarek and Christina had grown much closer since he'd stepped away from their relationship. Marc was happy for them, even as his loneliness increased with each passing season.

He wanted what they had.

He wanted a woman of his own. A woman he didn't have to share. But given the laws and reality of their world, that wasn't going to happen. Marc had resigned himself to a life alone as there was no way he could go back to sharing their bed once a week, as was custom.

Opening his eyes, he glanced around the great hall in Castle Garen. Many of their neighbors had come to celebrate the birth and naming ceremony of the new child. All four Bakra brothers were there with their wives. He watched them carefully, sensing no strife or unease amongst the couples. They all seemed happy in their lives, sharing one woman between two brothers.

In fact, all the people around him seemed happy. And he was happy too. This was a joyous occasion but, underlying it all, he felt as if something in his life was lacking. Amidst the crowd of people, he felt utterly alone.

Shaking off the mood, he gripped the ale-filled chalice in his hand and rose. "To Jarek and Christina and their new girl child, Allina. May health and happiness be with them always."

The crowd cheered and raised their glasses in a toast. Christina smiled at him before returning her attention to the baby. Jarek stared hard at him, as if sensing his unsettled thoughts.

Lowering his cup to the table, he turned and strode from the room, unable to stand the happy throng any longer. His long legs ate up the distance as he headed up the stone staircase that led to the family quarters. When he reached his room, he shoved open the door and strode inside, kicking it closed with his booted foot.

"What is wrong with me?" He raked his fingers though his hair as he paced back and forth. The fireplace was empty but he felt no need to strike a flint and light the waiting logs. No amount of heat could melt the icy numbness that filled him more each day.

The only time relief came was when he slept. He stopped at the window and peered out at the stars that were just beginning to wink into view as darkness claimed the land. He'd been dreaming of a woman for the past two nights now. His fingers wrapped around the hilt of the sword strapped to his waist and tightened. In the dream, the woman was his. She was in danger and he was unable to protect her. To a warrior, that was unacceptable.

But there were other moments in his dreams. Hot, tender moments. He whirled away from the window and stalked to a large wooden chair which sat in front of the fireplace. Throwing himself into it, he tilted back his head and closed his eyes, trying to recapture the vision of this woman.

She was tall, with long, slender legs that seemed to go on forever. He grunted and adjusted his pants to relieve his growing erection. It didn't help. Her hair was the color of fire and she seemed to favor keeping it confined at her nape. Marc longed to sift his fingers through her hair to see if was as soft as it appeared.

Her face was heart-shaped and her nose was slender and feminine. Her skin was flawless except for six freckles, which dotted her otherwise pale complexion—three on either side of her nose. Stubbornness showed in the slight upward tilt of her angular chin. She'd be a handful and then some.

Sighing, he clasped his hands over his stomach and willed sleep to come. Maybe she would come to him in his dreams again and fill the lonely places in his heart. His breathing deepened and his head lolled to one side…

~ ~ ~ ~ ~

He stood at the bottom of the bed and watched her sleep. Her hair was down but it was too dark for him to see more than the occasional glint of red. The light seeping in through the window was slight but it was enough. For now.

He sensed two others in the room and squinted to see into the darkness. The figures slid from the darkness to stand on either side of him, poised and ready to fight to protect her.

"She is mine." His words were little more than a low growl. Every muscle in his body tensed and he forced himself to relax. He bent his knees slightly and fingered the sword at his waist. He was coiled, ready to fight for what was his.

He'd been drawn to Christina from the moment he'd laid eyes on her but this was different. It went deeper, all the way to his very soul. The woman on the bed had been made especially for him, belonged to him. Nothing would stand in the way of him claiming her.

Both men paused and watched him. He sensed they weren't afraid to fight him but were rather trying to decide what to make of him. Finally, the one on his left gave a curt nod. "Kathryn is ours as well." The voice was rough and Marc could hear the underlying challenge. So be it. He glanced over at the other man who inclined his head slightly.

A low moan came from the bed, pulling all their gazes to the woman who lay there. The moonlight on her face revealed her frown. Tension seemed to fill the air around them. Her brow wrinkled and she held out her hands as if to ward them off. "No," she gasped, batting her hands uselessly at the air.

Marc's heart ached for her obvious pain. Unable to stop, he unsheathed his sword and put it aside, before crawling onto the bed beside her. "Hush," he crooned as he cupped the side of her face with his hand.

Her eyelids fluttered and she blinked at him. "Who?" she gasped.

He didn't give her time to object but gently laid his lips against hers. They were soft and warm and tasted sinfully sweet. He felt the mattress sink on either side and knew the other two men were moving in to stake their claim.

Ignoring them, he focused all his attention on the woman in the bed. Kathryn, they'd said her name was. "Open for me, Kathryn." His tongue traced the seam of her lips, coaxing her to part them. Her name rolled easily from his mouth and he liked the sound of it.

Her hand clutched at his shoulder and she sighed. "Dreaming," she muttered. Marc took advantage and slid his tongue into the moist cavern of her mouth. He slid his tongue over hers, inviting it to play with his. After a moment's hesitation, she did just that. Marc's pants were uncomfortably tight now, his erection pressing hard against the leather but he didn't care. He could lie here all night long and just taste her mouth.

Her fingernails dug into his shoulders and he pulled free long enough to push aside his leather vest, letting it fall to the mattress behind him. "Touch me." It was part demand, part plea and she answered it. Flattening her palms against his skin, she stroked over the hard planes of his chest. He swore under his breath when her fingers brushed his nipples. His cock was throbbing hard now and his balls ached.

"My turn." The sound came from the other side of Kathryn. The dim light shone on the man watching them. His hair was dark, his body lean and determination was etched on every inch of his face. There was no doubt that this man wanted Kathryn.

As Marc watched, the dark-haired man leaned down and kissed her lightly, sipping at her lips. "Tienan," she groaned before turning her head away. "Logan?"

Her voice was little more than a whisper but the man behind him heard it. He pushed Marc aside and cupped her face in his hands. "I'm here, little one."

Marc shifted until he sat between her legs, her nightgown bunched around her thighs. "Kathryn?" Her name was low and urgent. He needed her to look at him, to acknowledge him.

She turned to him and frowned. "Who are you?"

"I am Marc of the House of Garen—" He broke off as she gasped.

"You came. I wanted to dream of you and you came." She smiled at him then and it went straight to his heart and his groin.

He placed his hands on her legs and slid them upward, pushing the light fabric of her gown higher and higher until she was exposed to him. He wished he could see her better, wanted to know if the fine hair between her thighs was as fiery red as that on her head.

Her legs shifted restlessly against the mattress and he pressed them wide as he bent forward. "You smell hot and sweet," he muttered. "How will you taste?"

She didn't answer but she made no move to stop him as he licked up one side of her labia and down the other. Her low moan was music to his ears. He raised his head and smiled, noting that the two other men had shifted the straps of her gown from her shoulders and were sucking on her nipples.

Her hips tilted upward and he feathered his fingers over her sensitive flesh before slowly pressing one inside her opening. She was snug and hot around him. His body clenched as he imagined how tightly her pussy would hold his cock, squeezing it in exquisite sensual torture as he fucked her.

He shoved his hips into the mattress and pressed down hard. He was close to coming, could feel the liquid seeping from the tip of his shaft. His balls were heavy and pulled up tight against his body. His skin was slick with perspiration as he struggled not to yank down his pants and shove his cock into her welcoming heat.

He needed her pleasure first.

She made a sound of displeasure when he withdrew his finger but cried with delight when he pressed two fingers back into her. Her moist walls closed around him, pulling him deeper. Leaning closer, he inhaled her unique scent—musky, aroused woman with a touch of honey and something floral. It went to his head harder and more quickly than the most potent of ale.

He widened his fingers and withdrew slowly, keeping the tips of his fingers just inside her sheath. Then he plunged them back inside. Over and over, he repeated the action, gaining speed as he went.

Her hips were arching into the air, her body jerking. He knew she was close to reaching her pleasure. He captured the bundle of nerves at the apex of her sex between his lips and sucked. Kathryn screamed his name as she came. Satisfaction roared through him as he continued to stroke her with his hand and his mouth, prolonging her climax.

Finally, he forced himself to release her. Sitting back, he swiped his face with the back of his hand, groaning when her scent filled his nostrils. His hands went to the fastenings of his pants. He would have her now.

"Kathryn?" She blinked at him, hearing the question. It was her choice. Logan and Tienan sat on either side of her, watching her, waiting for her decision.

She nodded. "I asked the tapestry to bring you to me and it did."

Marc's fingers froze on the laces of his pants. "Tapestry?"

She gifted him with a sleepy, sated smile. "Yes, tapestry. I read the book and know all about Jarek, Christina and Javara. I've wanted you since I first read the story." She sighed. "I found the book months ago but only discovered the tapestry and an old journal in the attic this afternoon. I asked for it to bring you to me in my dreams." She laughed. "I needed this release more than I thought." She glanced, almost shyly, at the men on either side of her. "Although, I didn't imagine all three of you."

Marc's head began to spin, his vision fading. "No. This can't be." He could hear the horror in his voice as the room around him began to disappear.

"Marc." He could hear the fear in her voice, hear the exclamations of the other two men. He managed to roll to one side and grab his sword…

~ ~ ~ ~ ~

He jerked awake, jumping to his feet, sword drawn, his hand clenched tightly around the handle. Kathryn's cry seemed to echo in the air around him. He was painfully aroused, his erection pulsing heavily.

"A dream." He shook himself, stumbling over to the table and pouring himself a cup of water. "It was only a dream." He downed it in one gulp.

A strange scent caught his attention and he raised his hand to his nose. "Impossible." He sniffed again and sure enough, the smell of musk, honey and flowers drifted up from his fingers. His cock flexed and he swore, loosening the ties of his pants to alleviate the pressure.

He shook his head and raked his waist-length brown hair back from his face. "It's all the thoughts of Christina and Jarek that made me dream of the tapestry." The hairs on the back of his neck were warning him of danger but he couldn't see anything out of place in the room.

He lowered his sword, placing it back in the scabbard at his side. It was only then that he realized he was no longer wearing his vest. He glanced around the room but it was nowhere to be seen.

* * * * *

Kathryn cried out, bolting upright in the bed. A large hand covered her mouth, drowning out most of her scream as the light on her bedside table came on. Tienan and Logan, both looking disheveled, were seated on either side of her, concern in their eyes.

Tienan slowly lowered his hand. "Are you all right?"

Her eyes darted around the room, assuring her that there was no one else beyond the three of them here. "I'm fine. It was just a dream."

Logan gave a rough chuckle. "Dreams can be pretty powerful things." He shifted on the bed and it was then she noticed his erection. She took a quick peek at Tienan and noted he was in the same condition. Her own body pulsed and ached and she could feel liquid release between her thighs. It had been one heck of a realistic dream.

It was only then that she realized that the straps of her gown were down around her elbows, exposing her breasts and the bottom of it was bunched around her waist. Thankfully, the blankets were covering her but her shoulders were still bear. Both men were watching her carefully and she could see the heat of arousal in their eyes.

She cleared her throat. "Yes, they can. Sorry if I woke you."

"That's okay. I was dreaming too but it ended abruptly." Tienan's gaze narrowed as the cover slipped down one arm. "What the hell is that?" He grabbed the blanket and shoved it aside.

Kathryn cried out and tucked the cover around her exposed breasts. "What is the matter with you?"

"Oh, sweetheart." Logan's soft words were tinged with anger and sadness. She glanced at him but he was looking at her arm.

She swallowed hard, realizing that the bruises from today's interrogation were fully visible. They were even worse than earlier—dark and ugly. "It's nothing."

"I'm going to kill him." There was no need for either of them to ask who Tienan meant. They all knew that General Caruthers was responsible.

"No." Reaching out, she cupped his face in her hands. "That's suicide and I couldn't bear it if anything happened to you." She looked at Logan. "To either of you."

Letting out a rough breath, Tienan rested his forehead against hers. "I cannot let him live. I have sworn to protect you. You risked everything for me, for us."

"You can let him live. For now, anyway. All that matters is finding a way for all of us to escape the city and get beyond the Gate."

"All of us?" Logan sat very still beside her.

Releasing Tienan, she turned to him, licking her lips. She had the weirdest feeling that she knew what his kiss would taste like, what both their kisses would taste like. That was one heck of a realistic dream she'd had. Forcing it to the back of her mind, she focused on the task at hand — keeping all of them alive.

"All of us. I can't stay here. Not now."

"There is no safety for you beyond the Gate." Tienan took her hand, wrapping his fingers around hers. "You should stay here."

Kathryn shook her head. "I'd rather die out there, than stay in here and be party to more atrocities."

Logan started to protest but she held up her hand. "My mind is made up. Either I go with you or I go alone."

"With us," Tienan declared. "You will not be alone."

"Okay then, it's time to try to get some sleep." She tugged at the straps of her gown, pulling them back into place. Reaching down, she pushed the fabric back over her torso and legs. Her hand hit something and she frowned as she dragged it from under the covers. "What the heck?" A large, leather vest emerged from beneath the blankets, held tight in her grasp.

Logan frowned and then his eyes widened. "The dream."

"What do you mean?"

Tienan's eyes narrowed and he scowled at the garment before shooting Logan a look that she couldn't interpret. "We'll talk more in the morning. Now is not the time."

Logan nodded once and then turned out the light, plunging the room back into darkness. She expected both men to return to their pallets on the floor. Instead, they stretched out on either side of her in a protective barrier.

Kathryn pulled the vest close to her chest and inhaled the masculine scent. She had no idea how it had gotten in her bed. Maybe it actually belonged to either Tienan or Logan. She didn't think so, but then, she didn't know what was in the knapsack they'd brought with them when they escaped.

Had she found it in the attic and brought it down with her? She was so distracted these days that anything was possible. Maybe she'd wanted the fictional Marc to be real, so she'd used this prop to try to imagine it.

Yes, that must be it. Her emotions and thoughts were all a muddle the past few days and that was no surprise. The stress and tension must be getting to her worse than she thought. Still, she pulled the leather close to her heart before she snuggled beneath the covers. With her protectors on either side of her, she slept.

Chapter Three

ฌ

As he strode down the steps to the great hall for breakfast the next morning, Marc was still unsettled by the realistic dream from the night before. He could feel the smoothness of feminine skin beneath his fingers, taste her sweet lips and smell the perfume of her arousal. "Kathryn." He whispered her name, savoring the sound of it.

He hadn't slept much last night, instead tossing and turning as he relived every single moment he'd spent with her over and over again. His cock began to stir and he groaned. He'd been forced to give himself some relief during the night but it certainly hadn't helped beyond the moment. He was still aroused and hungry.

The only problem was that the woman he wanted was only a figment of his dreams. He still hadn't found the missing vest but was trying not to dwell on it. Maybe he'd taken it off before he'd fallen asleep in the chair and a servant had sneaked in and taken it to be cleaned. That was the logical explanation. He had several vests, so there was no need for him to be concerned. It had been a dream. Nothing more. The tapestry had already been here twice in this generation and that was one more time than was normal. Wanting his dream woman to be true did not make her so.

Although he still didn't understand why there had been two strange men in the dream. If he'd had his way, he'd have been alone with her. But, dreams were what they were. The men had probably been there because, in Javara, no man had a woman to himself, so he expected to share her. That was enough of an explanation to suit him for now.

Jarek was already seated in his customary chair at the head of the family table, which was on a slightly raised dais with all the other tables perpendicular to it. Extra tables had been added for the three-day feast. Last night was just the beginning. There would be competitions and food aplenty for the next two days.

Christina spotted him first as she placed a large platter of food on the table and waved him over. "Come sit and talk with us."

He strode toward her and offered her a smile. "Good morning." Bending down, he placed a chaste kiss on her cheek. Sliding into the seat beside hers, he helped himself to a slice of the thick, brown bread and slathered it with honey. He wasn't really hungry but knew that not to eat was to invite unwanted questions.

"I'll just help Mara in the kitchen." Christina shot him a worried look before hurrying off. He knew then that there was no escaping the coming confrontation with his brother.

"Marc," Jarek began. "You have not been happy these past months."

He stared at Jarek, trying to figure out a way to explain how he felt that would not make his brother feel responsible in any way. Jarek was dressed as he was, in leather pants, boots and vest. They both wore thick bronze arm and wristbands and a four-foot sword sat in a scabbard at their waists. They were similar in build but their coloring was different. Jarek's hair was black, while his was dark brown. His brother's eyes were brown, while his were more golden in color. But the differences were more than just physical. In the past six years, Marc sensed a deepening contentment in his brother that had not existed before Christina came into his life. He was happy for his brother but he felt a growing restlessness inside himself.

"I have not been unhappy," he began.

N.J. Walters

Jarek slammed his fist down onto the table in a rare show of temper. The plates and cutlery all shook and clattered and Marc had to grab the cup in front of him to keep it from falling over. "You are my brother. Do you think I do not know that you are feeling restless and unsettled? Do you think I have not noticed that it has been a year since you sought out Christina and our bed?"

Marc shook his head, setting the cup back on the table before facing Jarek. "I cannot." It was as simple and as complicated as that. "I do not belong there. Christina is yours. She has always been yours." He held up his hand to silence his brother. "Do not deny what is the truth. Christina has feelings for me but they are the feelings a woman has for a brother, not a lover. Everything was fine at first but changed when she gave birth to Baron. We both know he is my son." The boy's coloring was exactly as Marc's—brown hair and golden eyes.

The words Marc had never spoken were now there in front of them. Jarek sighed and nodded. "I know," he whispered softly. "But he is the son of my heart. He is mine."

Marc nodded, forcing himself not to rub his chest as the old ache arose. "I know but I will not have another child I cannot claim."

He heard a stifled cry behind him and whirled around in his seat. Christina stood there, her hand over her mouth, her face white. "Christina." He pushed out of his chair and came to his feet, taking a step toward her. "There is nothing for you to be concerned about."

"Nothing for me to be concerned about?" She repeated his words back to him, a frown forming on her face as she fisted her hands by her side. "How can you say that? I know you've been unhappy for such a long time now. How can I make it better?"

His heart began to pound heavily in his chest. How he adored this woman. In fact, he loved her, but not in the way he had when she'd first arrived. Now he knew she was his brother's woman. Surprisingly, he'd come to terms with it

32

quite easily. It didn't make being alone any easier but it was what it was. None of them could change how they felt.

"Come here." He opened his arms to her and she gave a small cry before flinging herself into them. Closing them around her, he hugged her tightly, lowering his head so he could whisper in her ear. "You cannot change the fact that you love Jarek. No," he held her in his grip when she started to pull away. "It is the way it is supposed to be, Christina. You were never mine." He paused. "Well, maybe you were mine for a few months but that is all. And now the way I love you is different. I know you understand."

This time when she pulled away, he let her. Her blue eyes were luminous with unshed tears and one of them trickled down her cheek. She dashed it away with the back of her hand. "I don't know what to do."

"There is nothing to do. I want you and Jarek to be happy. You have three healthy, beautiful children and you will have more. You will raise them and I will be their doting uncle." He offered her a smile before looking over her head at his brother.

Jarek was watching them, concern etched on his face but Marc sensed the resignation as well. Good. He wanted them both to accept his feelings and embrace their life together without worrying about him.

A noise drifting in from the entryway had him stepping in front of Christina to shield her from whoever was coming. The guests had set up large, ornate tents in the courtyard for their comfort and privacy, as the castle could not accommodate all of them. The voices became distinct as the Bakra brothers and their wives came into view, followed closely by the Fairmount brothers. The day was starting and the guests were arriving for breakfast. The quiet family time was over.

"I'll go tell Mara we need to start serving our guests." He turned his head but Christina was already on her way to the kitchen.

Appetite gone, he shot his brother a look.

"Give her time. This situation is not easy on any of us." Jarek rose from his seat to meet his guests. "She feels as if she has failed us somehow."

Pain shot through Marc. "There is no need for her to think that. This is no one's fault."

Jarek nodded. "I know. But that does not make it any easier on any of us."

"I'm going riding. I'll be back in time for the competitions later." With that, he turned on his heel and strode from the room, calling a greeting to his friends and their wives as he left.

He went straight to the stables and saddled his horse. Man and beast were as one as they galloped over the countryside but no matter how far they ran, a growing restlessness filled Marc. Something was coming but he didn't know what. He could feel it in his bones.

By the time he returned, the courtyard was filled with men and women enjoying the various skills competitions that had been set up as entertainment. Many of the men called to him, taunting him good-naturedly as he strode into the castle. His brother was engaged in a sword fight but made quick work of his competition when he saw Marc. Saluting his fallen opponent, he accepted the congratulations of the men around him.

Marc knew his brother would be close behind him, so he took the stairs two at a time and hurried to his room. He just needed a moment alone before he joined the crowd. He'd barely shut the door behind him when there was a low tap. It couldn't be Jarek. His brother wouldn't bother to knock.

"Come," he called as he plucked a leather thong off the mantle and began to wrap it around his hair at the nape. He needed it out of the way if he was going to compete.

The door was pushed open and Christina stood just outside, a tray in her hands. "I thought you'd be hungry. You didn't eat much breakfast." She looked beautiful as always, with her waist-length blonde hair flowing free and a dark blue gown clinging to every curve. As a man, Marc could appreciate her beauty but it no longer did anything for him sexually.

"Thank you." He motioned her inside, not liking the way she hesitated. "There is no need for you to knock at my door, Christina. You are always welcome."

She gave him a tiny smile and came forward, placing the tray on the table in front of the fireplace. "We're okay, aren't we?" She shifted from one foot to the other and plucked unconsciously at the lacing on her dress.

Hair tied back, Marc came forward and cupped her face in his hands. Christina had a beautiful spirit. His brother was a very lucky man. "Yes." He kissed her forehead. "There is nothing to be concerned about."

He knew his brother was standing in the doorway watching them. Raising his head, he nodded slowly. Jarek nodded back. They knew that everything had changed but they would be fine. They were family.

"What's this?" Christina pulled away from him and walked over to the end of the bed. She gasped and began to sway. "No, it can't be." He could hear the horror in her voice as he rushed toward her.

Marc reached her side just a step ahead of Jarek. A dusty bundle sat atop the fur coverings of his bed. He put his hand out.

"Don't touch it," she yelled before burying her face against her husband's chest. "It's *the* tapestry."

"Impossible." Marc picked up the fabric and shook it out. "It's probably just an old tapestry from the castle. Although I don't know why it's here." His voice tapered off as the image came into view. Before his very eyes, the tapestry changed, the dust disappeared and the jewel-toned colors became crisp and sharp. Castle Garen was easily recognizable, along with the lone man standing in front of it. Him.

"Marc?" He could hear the edge of terror in his brother's voice. Asking the question none of them dared to speak aloud. Had the tapestry come to take Christina away?

"Get her away from here." Marc strode to the far end of the room, his eyes still fixed on the tapestry, which was changing again. He could hear Jarek and Christina calling to him but their words were lost as he became enthralled with the piece of fabric in his hands.

The image distorted and the castle disappeared, replaced by a large home unlike anything he'd ever seen. It was made of wood and brick and didn't look very sturdy to his eyes. The image was dark and the world around it a dangerous place. In the center of the fabric was a woman. But not just any woman.

Her. His woman. The woman from his dreams.

Her red hair was tucked into some kind of knot but the color shone through. The longer he stared at the tapestry, the more sharply it came into focus. Her eyes were a brilliant green and he could see the intelligence in them. Her skin was flawless and her lips begged to be kissed.

A low growl came from the back of his throat as the figures of two men coalesced beside her. The men from the dream. The men who wanted her as much as he did. No! No one could want her as much as he did.

"Take me to her," he ordered the tapestry before holding it close to his heart. Jarek stood in front of Christina, sword drawn, ready to fight. He could have told his brother there was no need to worry. The tapestry had not come for Christina.

It had come for him.

But words were impossible as the room began to spin around him. A bright light blinded him and he felt his body being ripped away from his home. Christina screamed. His brother roared but Marc felt nothing but a sense of rightness.

He was going to claim his destiny and his woman.

* * * * *

Kathryn was out of breath by the time she shoved open the door of her bedroom. A heavy hand fell on her shoulder and she barely kept from crying out as she was whirled around. She heard the door being closed and locked. That wouldn't help. It was too late.

"What is it?" Tienan released his grip on her shoulders and began to rub them instead.

"They're coming," she gasped. "My father, the General…" she waved her hand at the door.

Logan was already headed toward the secret entrance. "We have to move."

Kathryn dug into her large purse and pulled out two small but lethal handguns. "Here. This is all I could manage to get."

Tienan whistled softly as he took one of them and checked to make sure it was loaded. Flicking on the safety, he tossed it to Logan and then took the other one for himself, repeating his swift, sure motions before tucking it into the waistband of his jeans. "You stole these from the experimental lab."

It wasn't a question but she answered him anyway. "Yes. I knew it was over when General Caruthers came into the labs this morning. They questioned me again and then released me. I could tell that he knew something, that he was just playing cat-and-mouse with me." She slung the strap of her purse over her head and her right arm. This way her hands were free but she wouldn't lose it.

Tienan grabbed his pack and hustled her over to where Logan waited. "I didn't know what else to do. Maybe I should have just tried to brazen it out but when I got the chance I left and came home." She closed her eyes as a feeling of helplessness overwhelmed her. "I'm sorry."

"You have nothing to be sorry for," Logan assured her as he stepped into the tunnel ahead of her. It was dark but he had a flashlight that she'd taken from the kitchen several days ago.

Kathryn hated enclosed spaces but her fear of what was behind them was even greater than what was ahead. She plunged forward and Tienan followed close behind, shutting the secret entrance behind him. The darkness was complete, the only light from the flashlight.

She started to speak but Logan held up his hand, instantly silencing her. It was then she heard it. Voices coming from below. Shit! They knew about the tunnels. Panic welled up inside her, threatening her composure.

"I'm right here," Tienan whispered in her ear.

As suddenly as that, the fear was gone, replaced by an overwhelming sense of calm and determination. She'd fight beside these two men and die beside them if necessary. "We can't let them take us alive." That would be the worst thing that could happen to any of them. They would be brutally tortured for days on end, an example to anyone who thought to defy the Ruling Council. "Promise me." She placed a hand against each man, needing his word. "Don't let them take me."

"I promise." Tienan's voice was little more than a low rumble.

Satisfied, she turned to Logan. "What do we do?"

"Up, we have to go back." His face was solemn in the dim glow of the flashlight. "It's too easy for them to trap us here."

She twisted on the stairs and felt Logan's hand against the small of her back as they charged back up the stairs and into her bedroom. "If we can get to the west wing, there's another secret set of stairs. Maybe they don't know about that one."

Logan shut the door and dragged a sofa in front of it. It wasn't much but it would slow them down.

"It's too late." Tienan dumped his pack onto the floor and forced her into a corner behind him, placing his larger body in front of her as he drew his gun and focused on the door. "They're here."

The bedroom door burst open and two armed men surged into the room, their weapons trained on the interior. Neither Logan nor Tienan hesitated. Two shots later the soldiers were dead on the floor.

"How long will your ammunition last?" a male voice questioned. Kathryn's throat tightened. The General was here.

"Long enough to shoot you, you cowardly bastard. Just show your head in the doorway and I'll take care of that little chore." Logan plastered his body against the side of a large chest of drawers, letting the bulk of it shelter him.

"Ah, Logan." The General chuckled. "You always were a hothead. Such emotion. You're the main reason the project needs to be terminated. Tienan is much more levelheaded. A thinker." His tone changed, becoming hard. "Tienan, you have been deemed a success. Eliminate the two traitors beside you and you'll be spared."

Kathryn jerked her head around to look at Tienan. He never flinched, never moved, his arm extended, gun pointed toward the door.

Logan laughed but the sound was anything but pleasant. "If you think either of us believe one word coming out of your lying mouth, I've got some land beyond the Gate I can sell you."

"See, that's why you're being terminated," General Caruthers taunted. "Your emotions always get the better of you, Logan. You're a follower, not a leader. You won't take a piss without Tienan's permission."

Logan's finger tightened almost imperceptibly on the trigger but other than that, he didn't move. Kathryn knew that both men could maintain their positions for hours without tiring. After all, it was what they'd been trained to do.

Another group of soldiers burst into the room and the men fired. Blood splattered and cries of anguish rang out as the men fell to the floor. Kathryn buried her face against Tienan's back, not wanting to see the carnage that now littered her bedroom.

"You got any more bullets for these things, sweetie?" Logan's whisper was so low she barely heard him.

She shook her head. "I tried…" There had been no time to get more. She'd barely gotten the weapons.

"Oh well." He shrugged and tossed the gun aside. In a move so fast it was a blur, Logan dove and rolled, grabbing a weapon from one of the dead soldiers. A barrage of bullets hit the floor beside him as he continued to roll. Somehow he not only managed to return fire but kicked another weapon close enough for Tienan to swoop down and grab it.

For several long minutes, the walls and floors were peppered with gunfire. Tienan shoved her up against the bed, using the bulk of the piece and the mattresses to shield them. Silence reigned as the dust settled. A feather flew past Kathryn's nose. Her pillows were in shreds.

"Kathryn, we know that this is all their doing. They brainwashed you into helping them. They're smart and trained to manipulate a naïve woman like yourself. Did they tell you they loved you? Did they sleep with you?" She wanted to cover her ears. Instead, she forced herself to listen to her father as he continued. "You'll have to be punished but then you can go back to work in the lab. Everything will be the way it was."

Tienan stiffened beside her. She ignored him as she tossed her answer back at her father. "Do you think I'm that stupid? The only reason you want me back is because I'm the best scientist you've got." There was no conceit in her words—it was fact. "You're more replaceable than I am and that sticks in your craw, old man. Always has."

"You ungrateful little bitch. I should have killed you when I took care of your weak, sniveling mother. I can see that you have too much of her genetics in you."

Kathryn gasped and Tienan gripped her arm and shook her, pulling her back down beside him. She hadn't even realized that she'd started to stand up.

"Enough. The bullets are gone in those guns you managed to take. There is no way out for any of you."

Kathryn glanced over to the far wall where Logan was hunkered down behind a large armoire. She gave a small moan when she saw the patch of red on his arm. He looked at her and gave her thumbs up. Fists pounded on the secret door but so far the lock had held. Unless they knew where to find the latch, they'd have a hard time opening it. It wasn't much but it bought them some extra time.

There was some activity just beyond the door and then a line of four men walked into the room, holding shields in front of them. General Caruthers stepped in behind them, followed by her father.

"The time has come to give yourselves up." She could hear the underlying glee in the General's voice and shivered.

Turning to Tienan, she gripped his arm. "You promised me."

His eyes were sad as he leaned forward and kissed her softly on the lips. "I know. Turn around."

She knew he couldn't look into her eyes and kill her. Instead, she focused on Logan, blowing him a kiss. Her fingers dug into the leather strap of her purse. Tienan's hands tightened around her throat. She tensed and then forced herself to relax.

The General, realizing their intent, yelled. "Stop!"

Just then a brilliant light flashed in the room. For a second, Kathryn wondered if this was what it felt like when you died. But the moment passed and she was still very much in this world. She blinked and half stood, unable to believe her eyes.

A giant of a man stood just beyond the door, a tapestry in one hand and a four-foot sword in the other.

"Kill the men. Spare the woman," the General ordered. "She's mine."

The man took in the room at a glance, his eyes widening when he saw her. Swiftly, he turned back to the threat and attacked. His great sword cut through the men like a hot knife through butter. As she watched, two bloody heads rolled toward the bed. Using the distraction to their advantage, both Tienan and Logan dove for the other weapons, bringing them up and firing. Both her father and the General dove through the door but they weren't in time. She heard her father screaming in pain and the General yelling at him to shut up.

The stranger swung around and leapt over the bed, landing by her side. "You are unhurt?"

His accent was strange but she understood him perfectly. "Yes." She raised her hands to his face. He seemed so familiar. She blinked, taking in his bare chest, the arm and wristbands and the long brown hair that fell down his back. "Marc?" This was impossible. Marc was nothing but a character from a book, a figment from her dreams.

He flashed her a grin. "Kathryn."

"I hate to break up this little party but we've still got trouble." Tienan had a weapon in each hand, one pointed at the secret entrance, the other at the door. It was only then that she heard the commotion on the other side of the tunnel and saw the door move. They were starting to break through. Logan was beside him in a similar position.

Marc stared at them, his golden-brown eyes narrowing. "You are the men from the dream." They both nodded.

Shock filled her. "That was just a dream. That wasn't real."

Marc used the tip of his sword to pluck the remains of the brown vest from the bed. It had been damaged in the shootout. "I believe this is mine."

"This can't be happening," she moaned, rubbing her temples.

"It can and it is. Choose." He glanced sharply at both men. "Stay here and die or come with me. I don't know if the tapestry will take us all but we can try."

"The tapestry." She grabbed it from Marc's grasp and shook it out. Sure enough, it was the same tapestry from the attic, yet different. Her family home filled the fabric but as she watched, it faded, replaced once again by the castle that had been there originally.

Marc wrapped his arm around her, pulling her so close she could hear the steady thud of his heart against her ear. His sword was held in front of them, a protective measure. She felt surrounded by his strength and strangely safe in spite of the shouts, the pounding of feet and the smell of death in the air.

"Stay or leave." It took her a second to realize Marc was talking to Tienan and Logan. Held tight in his arms, she didn't doubt that she was going with him. She held out her hands to them. They glanced at one anther and took a step forward, each of them grasping a hand.

"Hold on tight and do not let go," Marc warned them.

The secret entrance was shoved open and men started to pour through. Kathryn closed her eyes, knowing they were all dead. It was too late.

A blinding light flashed and she heard Tienan cry out. His grip faltered but she clung tightly, refusing to let go of either of them. With Marc's arm banded tight around her, she felt her body being torn away from the room, from the world she knew.

Then there was only darkness.

Chapter Four

৪০

Marc bit back a groan as he tried to clear the fogginess from his brain. He was on his back, the hard surface beneath him stone. There was a weight on his chest—a soft, supple, shifting weight. Blinking, he glanced down and stilled.

Kathryn.

Everything came flooding back to him—his flight through time and space, the fight and their desperate escape. The only question was, where were they? Had they made it back to Javara?

He could see a window, the shutters thrown back and its colored glass panes visible. He turned his head slowly and relaxed as the familiar confines of his room met his gaze. The fireplace was cold but he recognized the oak table and the two large, carved chairs that sat beside it. Above the hearth hung a large ornate sword that had belonged to his father. He was home.

He turned his head in the other direction and saw the corner of his large four-poster bed and the edge of a black boot. At least one of the men had made it. Kathryn moaned, drawing his immediate attention. She shifted and her pelvis ground against his, bringing her feminine heat up against his rock-hard erection. It seemed that no matter the situation, he wanted the woman in his arms.

Her hair had come loose from its knot and long tendrils rested across his chest. Fascinated by the fiery color, he lifted a strand and brought it to his face. It was soft and smelled of flowers. His chest tightened and his cock flexed.

Her eyelids fluttered and gradually opened. He watched, uncertain how she would feel about this turn of events. She seemed to know him, yet she had claimed he was not real. How could that be?

His erection continued to throb and he shifted slightly, trying to ease some of the pressure on his balls. She couldn't deny he was real any longer. Not with his shaft pulsing against her sex. Even through the layers of their clothing, he could feel her heat.

Her green eyes opened and she blinked several times. Her lashes, thick and long, brushed her cheekbones. Her brows were a reddish brown. Everything about her captivated him. He wanted to know all there was to know about her, to uncover each and every one her secrets. He wanted to strip her clothing from her and spend hours learning the curves and hollows of her body. He longed to bury himself in her heat and bring them both to completion.

"What?" she began and broke off. She jerked away suddenly and he grunted, barely managing to keep his manhood safe from harm as she rolled off him. The satchel she had around her chest smacked him in the head.

He sat up slowly, rubbing his head, not wanting to alarm her unnecessarily. "You are in my room, in Garen Castle."

She licked her lips and he noticed how plump and pink they were. "That's impossible. This place doesn't really exist."

"So you have said. Yet it is so." He wanted to kiss those lips but forced himself to look away. There was time for that later, once he'd taken stock of the situation.

The dark-haired man was lying facedown a few feet away from them. The other man was on his back, just beyond, one arm flung over his head. A pool of blood was rapidly forming beneath the first man.

Kathryn's gaze followed his and she gasped when she saw the blood. "Tienan," she cried, flinging herself toward the dark-haired man. Yanking the satchel over her head, she dumped it aside. "He must have been shot before we managed to get away." She faced Marc, her skin pale but determination on her face. "Help me."

He scooted over beside them and quickly turned Tienan onto his back. Blood seeped from a wound on his shoulder. It must have come from the strange weapons they'd held in their hands. He glanced around the room but saw no sign of them. For some reason, they hadn't made the trip. Marc was glad they hadn't. They were deadly and, from what he'd seen, you didn't even have to be close to your opponent for it to be effective.

"I need hot water." Kathryn glanced wildly around the room. "I need an operating room."

Marc frowned. "An operating room?"

"Oh God. I need to remove the bullet and stitch up his wound."

"You are a healer," he could hear the awe in his voice. Healers were rare and valued by all. His woman was indeed a treasure.

"I need a needle, threads, any medical tools and medicines you have on hand." She turned back to her friend, placing her fingers against his neck.

Marc bounded to his feet and strode to the door. Flinging it open, he let out a roar that was sure to bring people running. In the meantime, he went to the fireplace, crouched down and lit the kindling beneath the logs that lay waiting.

He heard the sound of cloth ripping and turned. Kathryn had torn Tienan's shirt open. As he watched, she whipped her top over her head. Folding the material, she placed it over the wound. She was still wearing a white garment with lace around the edges. A bra. He'd heard Christina describe the contraption on more than one occasion. It was pretty but it exposed far more than it hid. Her breasts weren't overly large but they were firm and high.

"Check Logan."

She didn't even look his way as she tossed the command over her shoulder. He knew she was worried about both men. Pulling his gaze from her breasts, he took the few steps necessary to bring him to Logan's side. Marc crouched down and inspected the still man's body. "His arm has a slight wound but it's already stopped bleeding. He doesn't seem to be hurt anywhere else."

Footsteps pounded on the stairs and Jarek bust into the room, sword drawn. Behind him almost a dozen warriors followed, including Zaren and Bador Bakra. They filled the room, all of them staring at the group sprawled on the floor.

"Get Mara and Christina. I need hot water, needles, thread and medicine." He gave them Kathryn's requirement quickly.

He heard her gasp. She swayed slightly but her hold on the bandage never wavered. "This is crazy. Maybe I'm dead. Or maybe the General caught me and this is some delusion brought on by torture."

Jarek stepped forward, sword still held high. "What is going on?" The tone of his voice suggested that he wanted an immediate answer.

Marc sighed, knowing all hell was about to break loose. "The tapestry brought them."

Kathryn kept up the pressure on Tienan's wound as she glanced over at Logan. She'd seen him move the slightest bit a moment ago and knew he was awake but playing possum until he understood the situation. Although the guns were nowhere in sight, she knew he didn't necessarily need them to defend himself. Both he and Tienan had trained in martial arts and ancient weaponry. In fact, both men would probably enjoy swinging one of those swords that Marc carried.

She was losing her mind. There was no other explanation. She didn't want to look by the door, didn't want to face the large group of warriors, all armed, all talking at once. As soon as Marc had mentioned the tapestry, everything had changed.

She could sense the excitement bubbling beneath the tension. Would they attack or would they help?

She glanced at Marc and he seemed completely at ease but then again, this was his home, not hers. Not that she had a home anymore. Tienan gave a low moan, more of a sigh really and she leaned forward. "Don't move. You've got a bullet in your shoulder that has to come out."

He opened his eyes and they were clear and alert. "Where are we?"

"I'm not really sure," she began.

"You are at Castle Garen in Javara." The big warrior who'd burst through the door took a step toward them. His sword was still in his hand but at least he'd lowered it to his side. It looked big and sharp and Kathryn quickly remembered the heads of the two guards that Marc had decapitated in one swing. Bile rose in her throat but she swallowed it back.

Had they made a mistake in coming here? Not that they'd really had any choice in the matter. At least now they had a chance.

"I am Jarek." His brown eyes narrowed as he studied them.

Kathryn shook her head. This was unbelievable and it was just like in the book. Except this seemed real. She could see the family resemblance between him and Marc. His coloring was slightly different but the facial features were similar. And just like in the book, his hair fell to his waist with two thin braids framing his face. All the people around them seemed real. She knew that the blood seeping from Tienan was too real to be ignored.

"Kathryn Piedmont." She gave him a sharp nod.

Jarek took another step toward them, raising his sword the slightest bit. Both men beside her burst into action. Logan launched himself to his feet in one motion and delivered a kick to the midsection of another warrior who had been staring intently at her chest. When the man doubled over, Logan moved in swiftly, landed a karate chop on his arm and grabbed the sword from midair as it fell from the warrior's nerveless fingers.

Tienan wrapped his arm around her, rolling them both against the far wall. Pushing her behind him, he came to his feet, knees bent, arms loose by his sides, blood seeping heavily from his shoulder. She slapped the bandage back over the wound, ignoring his growl of protest. She wasn't letting him bleed to death. He could bitch at her later.

Logan placed himself in front of both Tienan and her. The large sword was gripped lightly in his right hand, his feet were braced apart and his knees were slightly bent. He was ready to fight. "You will not harm her."

She peeked around Tienan's shoulder, icy sweat rolling down between her shoulder blades. She shivered. She didn't want to die this way.

Marc was standing with his arms crossed, shaking his head. Jarek had lowered his sword, disbelief in his eyes. No one spoke.

"What's going on in here?" The woman stepped through the doorway and the men moved aside to let her into the room. Her hair was so blonde it was almost white and fell in a thick mass to her waist. Her figure was what could only be described as lush and she was carrying thick towels and some jars in her hands. She blinked, her eyes so blue that Kathryn thought that they couldn't be real.

The woman stopped beside Jarek and cocked her eyebrow at him. The warrior's face softened as he peered down at her. If Kathryn was correct, this would be Christina. The woman glanced at Logan and then beyond him, her gaze resting on Tienan. "You're injured." She turned back to her husband.

"We didn't do it," he grumbled. "The tapestry brought them."

Fear appeared in Christina's face and she took a step away from them. Marc rested his hands on her shoulders and Kathryn felt a flash of jealousy rock her to her core. It was as if she'd caught her man cheating on her. As if feeling her gaze on him, Marc looked her way and slowly removed his hands from Christina, letting them fall to his sides.

"The tapestry did not come for you, Christina." Marc reassured her. "It came for me."

Kathryn now understood the woman's fear. She obviously didn't want to return to her own time. This wasn't the time to start into some long explanation. "This is all fine and good," she spoke up, ignoring Tienan's low grunt of disapproval. "But Tienan is bleeding to death while we're gabbing." He was still steady in front of her but she could sense his waning strength.

Logan held the heavy weapon in front of him, the blade never wavering. "I will have your word that you will not harm Kathryn." She noted that he didn't mention his own wellbeing or Tienan's.

Christina's eyes widened. "They would never hurt a woman."

Her disbelief seemed to relax both men but Logan still didn't lower his sword. He had his eyes on Jarek, the obvious leader of the bunch.

"Women brought by the tapestry are special and are to be treated as such. No one will harm her here. The penalty for such a thing would be death." Jarek met Logan's gaze.

Marc strode forward, obviously reaching the limits of his patience. "Enough. Mara is outside the door with hot water and more supplies. If I'd wanted any of you dead, I would have left you all behind."

There was that. She tried to nudge Tienan forward but it was like trying to move a brick wall. She appealed to the only other sensible person in the room—the other woman. "You must be Christina." When the blonde woman nodded, Kathryn continued. "I'm Kathryn Piedmont. This is Tienan." She indicated him with a tilt of her head. "The man holding the sword is Logan. We come from Earth." That last line sounded like something out of a cheesy, twentieth century science fiction movie.

Christina's eyes widened and she smiled. "I'm from Earth originally too." Pushing past her husband, she strode forward. Logan stepped out of her way, uncertainty on his face. Kathryn knew he'd never raise a finger to hurt Christina. Slowly, he lowered the sword until the point was touching the stone floor.

Kathryn nodded. She'd known that from the book. "I think we come from vastly different times, though." Wrapping her free arm around Tienan's waist, she tried to take some of his weight on her. She could feel his muscles beginning to tremble.

"Bring him over here. We can talk more later." Christina motioned to Logan. "Help her move your friend to the bed."

Kathryn shook her head. "The table is better for surgery. He's got a bullet in his shoulder."

Christina became all business, directing the men to clear the table and move it closer to the fire. An older woman bustled into the room, carrying a large kettle of steaming water. Behind her, several men hefted an even larger kettle into the room, setting it over the fire.

The warriors all crowded around, no one leaving. Marc eased her gently aside and placed his hand over hers on the bandage. "I will hold it in place. See to your supplies."

She hated to leave Tienan but knew Marc was right. "Okay," she turned to Christina. "What do you have in medicines and medical supplies? I need a scalpel and something to act as forceps."

The women conferred and Kathryn quickly came to realize that Mara was the one with the knowledge. The woman offered up some herbal concoctions to speed healing and to deaden the area around the wound. As a botanist, Kathryn was intrigued by the salves. She definitely wanted to talk to Mara and pick her brain later.

Medical tools were harder to come by. There was no scalpel but plenty of sharp knives. When Christina explained what a scalpel was, Marc had drawn a wickedly sharp-looking dagger from a sheath just inside his boot and handed it to her. Kathryn quickly dropped it into the kettle to boil.

Her eyes fell on her purse and she grabbed it, ripping the zipper open. Digging into it, she found a small sewing kit with several thin needles and some thread. She knew she had a set of eyebrow tweezers in her makeup bag. They were small but they were better than nothing. She plunged the tweezers, thread and several needles into the pot of boiling water to sterilize them.

She also found a small bottle of aspirin, which would help with fever. Tienan was bound to have one. She only hoped that the medicine that Mara had would keep infection at bay. Right now, that was a bigger concern to her than removing the bullet. When she had everything she knew could be of help, she tossed the bag under the table for safekeeping.

"Okay." It was force of habit that had her reaching for the cuff of her blouse to roll it up. She muttered as she touched bare skin. She'd sacrificed her top as a bandage and she'd been running around in nothing but her bra ever since. Everyone had seen her this way. She muttered under her breath. There was nothing to be done about it and her bra was as decent as if she were wearing a bathing suit top for swimming.

Putting it out of her mind, she motioned for Mara to fill a bowl with hot water. She glanced at Tienan and noted the white lines of stress around his mouth and eyes. "How you holding up?"

"I'm good."

She heard the low grunts of approval from several of the men behind them and barely resisted rolling her eyes. Men! The stupidest things impressed them.

Kathryn tried to give him a reassuring smile. "This won't take long." Turning away, she began to focus on the job ahead.

A heavy hand landed on her shoulder. "What can I do to help?" Marc was a solid presence behind her. For some reason, just his being there steadied her, made her feel better. Which was crazy. He was a complete stranger. Still, she couldn't deny how he made her feel.

"I'll need you to hold his feet and legs. Logan will hold his shoulders."

Marc glanced at Logan. "I am bigger. I should take his shoulders."

She shook her head. "Both Logan and Tienan are much stronger than they look."

Turning aside, she blocked out everyone in the room. She plunged her hands in a basin of hot water Mara had poured from the smaller kettle she'd set beside the hearth, grabbed the bar of soap beside it and began to scrub. When her hands and arms were as sterile as she could get them, she shook off the water and let them air dry. One of Mara's helpers removed the dagger from the boiling water and handed it to her without touching the blade. The sterilized tweezers, needles and thread were laid out on a clean towel. It was a pitiful assortment of implements but it was all she had.

Bending over Tienan, she stared at the blood-saturated bandage. Logan had stripped away the remainder of Tienan's shirt. "Hold him." She waited until both men had moved into position and reached for the edges of the makeshift dressing. She didn't mean to look at Tienan but she couldn't help herself. He gave her a crooked smile and then closed his eyes.

Taking a deep, steadying breath, she peeled back the bandage and studied the wound. She dipped a cloth into a clean bowl of warm water and began to clean around the edges of the hole. Once that was done, she anointed the area with the salve that Mara assured her would help deaden the area. With nothing else to be done, she picked up the dagger and gripped it firmly but not too tight. Placing the tip on the edge of the wound, she began.

Time lost all meaning as she worked. First, she widened the hole and then came the arduous search for the bullet and fragments of cloth and bone that might have collected inside the wound. Her fingers cramped as she manipulated the tweezers, swearing under her breath whenever she lost a piece and had to try again.

Tienan's back arched when she made the first incision. But Logan held his shoulders on the table and Marc pressed down on his legs, not allowing him to move. Tienan never made a sound.

She knew he was still awake and aware of what was going on. Anyone else would have passed out by now but both Tienan and Logan had an extremely high tolerance for pain—another *gift* from their years of training. Mara worked alongside her, keeping the site clear of blood. From the sureness of her actions, it was obvious to Kathryn that the older woman had seen her share of bloody injuries.

When she stood for a moment and stretched out the kinks in her back, she felt Marc's large hand against her spine, rubbing it and lending her his strength. She turned her head toward him. He was watching her, his face calm but serious.

She went back to work, renewed. She didn't know how long it took her but finally she felt certain she had removed every piece of foreign matter. There had been several small bone chips, but thankfully, the bone itself was intact with no breaks or fractures. Given his genetics, Tienan would heal rapidly and with no serious complications. Or at least she hoped he would.

Picking up a bowl of hot water in which Mara had mixed something she guaranteed would keep the wound from becoming infected, Kathryn poured it over the wound, flushing it out.

When that was done, she picked up the threaded needle and began to place small, fine stitches in his flesh, closing the wound. The medicinal paste came next and she smeared it over his blotchy red, swollen skin and then placed a soft pad over it and wrapped strips of linen around his shoulder to keep it in place.

Mara worked tirelessly next to her, removing bloody and wet linen, replacing it with fresh and generally doing anything that Kathryn asked of her. The afternoon had waned as she'd worked and now candles blazed around her. Many of the warriors were standing around her makeshift operating table, holding a thick taper high, giving her the light she needed to work.

When she was done, Tienan opened his eyes. They were blurry with pain but he offered her a smile. "Thank you," he mouthed, no sound coming from his lips.

Kathryn felt a tear roll down her cheek. She raised her shoulder and swiped her face into it. She wasn't going to break down and cry in front of a room full of strangers. "No problem. Just don't make me have to do it again." Tienan's eyes were already shut tight, his breathing even. "Now he goes to sleep," she choked out. Turning aside, she plunged her hands in a bowl of tepid water and washed away as much of the blood as she could before grabbing a towel to dry them.

Logan released Tienan's shoulders and straightened. He reached out and pulled her into his arms, kissing the top of her head. "Thank you."

She patted his chest, feeling the steady beat of his heart. "You know there isn't anything I wouldn't do for the two of you."

He nodded, then released her.

"It was then she remembered that Logan had been wounded as well. "What about your arm?"

A lock of hair had come loose from her bun and he tucked it behind her ear. "It is nothing. I'll clean it later but it is already mending." She nodded, knowing that their genetics made them very fast healers.

Kathryn sensed Marc behind her and sighed. She wasn't ready to deal with the situation she now found herself in. She wanted to clean up and then she wanted to sleep.

Tired. She was so damn tired. Her life had been a pressure-packed tightrope walk for weeks now and her body was showing the strain. As if on cue, her stomach began to ache. And who the heck knew what a jump in time and space had done to her physiology. That is, if she truly believed that's what had happened.

At this point she didn't care.

Mara patted her on the arm before gently lifting Tienan's head and putting a pillow beneath it. "You did well. Get some food and rest. I'll watch over our patient." She glanced at Logan.

It was the "our" that did it for Kathryn. She knew that the older woman would care for Tienan. "Thank you. For everything," she added. Mara smiled and nodded as she draped the patient in a thick fur covering.

"I'll let you know if anything changes."

Kathryn handed her the bottle of aspirin. "If he wakes with a fever, give him three of these."

"Are you done?" Marc's voice was so close to her ear that she jumped.

"For now."

The words were barely past her lips when he swooped her off her feet and into his arms. She grabbed his shoulders for support as he turned. "What about Logan?"

"I'll be fine." He stood next to them, his gaze on Marc. "I'll watch over Tienan."

Some look passed between the two men that Kathryn couldn't understand and she was too damn tired to try to figure it out. Tomorrow. Tomorrow, she'd get the lay of the land and make a plan. Tonight she just wanted a bath and bed.

The men all stepped aside as Marc carried her toward the door. Only Christina stopped them. "I prepared the guest room at the end of the hall and left some clothing for Kathryn." She patted Kathryn's arm. "We'll talk in the morning. I'm sure you must have dozens of questions."

"Hundreds." Her voice slurred and she yawned. "Sorry."

Christina laughed. "Rest. There's plenty of time to get your answers. Tomorrow."

"Tomorrow," she agreed as Marc carried her out of the room.

As they left, she heard Jarek talking to Logan. "What was that move you used to disarm Mennoc?"

Chapter Five

ဆ

Marc carried his precious bundle down the hallway. Kathryn's head rested against his shoulder, her hand touching his chest. He was amazed at what he'd just witnessed. She'd stood there for hours, meticulously working to remove the chunk of metal, along with pieces of cloth and even bone from her friend. She'd never wavered, never flinched. Never mind that she'd been in the midst of a battle and then jumped to another world, she'd put her head down and done what needed to be done.

He was in awe of her courage.

He was also hard as a rock and desperate to claim her. For now, however, he was content to take care of her, doing what he needed to do. Once she was clean, fed and rested, he planned to seduce her. The corners of his lips turned upward at the thought of such a pleasant task.

"What are you smiling about?" Her words were slow and slurred, her eyes sleepy.

He shouldered his way into the guest room and kicked the door shut. Carrying her through the bedroom, he entered the small bathing chamber that was connected to it. Sure enough, steam rose from the water in the tub, a bar of soap sat ready on a low shelf and thick towels rested on a stool. Candles flicked, lending their glow to the room. "You need a bath."

"I must stink to the high heavens."

He frowned, seeing the self-conscious look in her eyes. Inhaling, he could still smell the light fragrance of flowers but it was overlaid by the stench of blood and sweat and the metallic tang of fear. "I thought it would relax you and make you feel better."

"It looks heavenly," she added as he released her legs, holding her steady as her feet touched the floor. "I'm okay." She stepped away, glancing over her shoulder at him.

He knew she expected him to leave but he wasn't going anywhere. Ignoring her disgruntled gaze, he studied the white garment binding her breasts. The bra seemed to close with hooks in the back. Reaching out, he slipped his fingers beneath the stretchy band and flicked the hooks. The garment parted easily. Marc smiled.

"Hey!" Kathryn whirled around, slapping her hands over her breasts. "What the heck do you think you're doing?"

"Helping you undress for your bath." He tried to hide his smile but he couldn't help himself. Even dirty and disheveled, she was the most beautiful woman he'd ever seen.

Her hair hung halfway down her back. Part of it was still pinned up but most of it had escaped and tumbled down long ago. There was a smudge of dirt on her cheek and blood stained the edges of her fingernails. His eyes narrowed as he noted the bruises on her upper arms. How had he missed those?

He held out his hand, gently stroking the dark blotches on one arm. "How did this happen?"

"It's not important." She glanced down at her feet and then raised her head to look him square in the face. "Look, I can't deal with all this now. I want a bath, some food and a bed."

"I agree." He dropped his hand and took a step closer. She took a step backward, the backs of her knees hitting the edge of the tub. "But I will know the truth." He glanced at the bruises on her arms and began to study the rest of her body. She was slender, almost too slender.

She held up one of her hands. "I can handle my own bath."

He took her fingers in his and brought them to his lips, kissing each individual knuckle. Her breath caught in her throat and he could feel the pulse in her wrist quicken. "I can help." He paused. "It's not as if I haven't seen you naked."

She pulled her hand away and scowled at him. "You most certainly haven't seen me naked."

"Are you forgetting the dream?"

"But that was just..." her words trailed off and she appeared uncertain. Kathryn shifted from one foot to the other. "That wasn't real."

"Yes, it was." Going to one knee in front of her, he began to unlace her shoe. "I touched your soft skin, tasted you." He paused long enough to kiss the inside of her knee. "Smelled your arousal." When it was done, he lifted her foot and pulled off the shoe. She grabbed the edge of the tub for support. She had to use both hands, which caused her bra to loosen, giving him a tantalizing peek of firm, white flesh.

"You mean you really touched me?" She licked her lips. He was sure it was an unconscious action but it set his blood racing through his veins. Her pupils dilated and her breathing quickened. She was becoming aroused by the memory, just as he was.

He removed her other shoe and laid it aside. Reaching up, he hooked his fingers in the straps of her bra and began to slowly slide them down her arms. "I know that your breasts fit the palm of my hand but I don't know what color your sweet nipples are."

Her arms relaxed by her sides and he tugged the bra off, tossing it over his shoulder. Her nipples were tight pink buds, begging to be touched. Tasted. Using his thumbs, he traced the edges, enjoying the sight of them tightening even more at his touch. Covering both mounds with his palms, he groaned.

He almost howled with pleasure when he felt her lean into his touch. It was the slightest of movements but he felt it all the same. His cock throbbed, an ache that only she could slake. He wanted to bury himself in her heated depths and never leave.

Sliding his hands downward, he traced his fingers over her ribcage, feeling the fragile bones beneath his palm. He frowned again. She was definitely too slender. Had she been ill?

She gasped as he stroked her stomach, his hands coming to rest on the button at the top of her pants. "Let me take care of you." He slipped the button from the hole. Grabbing the metal tab, he pulled it downward. Thanks to Christina, he knew what a zipper was. It was a fascinating contraption but right now it was simply one more impediment to getting Kathryn naked. More of her flesh came into view and he caught a glimpse of the edge of her underwear.

Pushing his hands inside, he couldn't resist giving her lush behind a squeeze before he shoved both pants and underwear down her thighs. Kathryn made a soft sound in the back of her throat but she didn't stop him. He quickly divested her of the rest of her clothing. When she was naked, he wrapped his arms around her waist, burying his face against the soft skin of her belly.

"I've tasted your honey. Traced the hot, slick folds of your pussy. Felt your inner muscles tightening around my fingers." His head was spinning as his breathing quickened. His cock was pressed so hard against the front of his pants that he was surprised the laces hadn't snapped.

He felt Kathryn begin to tremble. Swearing at himself, he bounded to his feet, picked her up and carefully lowered her into the tub. The water lapped at the edges as he released her. "You can say no to anything you don't like." He stroked a lock of fiery-red hair from her forehead. "Let me bathe you."

Kathryn almost moaned aloud. The man was seducing her with words alone. She was still having a hard time wrapping her mind around the fact that the dream she'd had was no dream but had actually happened. That meant that both Logan and Tienan had touched her as well. Seen her naked. It was enough to make her head spin. She wasn't quite sure how she felt about it.

On one hand, what woman didn't dream about being pleasured by three different men? If the book she'd found in the attic was to be believed, and at this point everything else had been accurate, then that kind of behavior was not only accepted but was expected in this world.

On the other hand, Kathryn didn't like the feeling that her life was spiraling out of control. She'd had more than enough of that over the past few months. She needed to think and to take charge of the situation.

But, a voice whispered in the back of her head, *what is the harm of taking some pleasure with Marc*? She'd dreamed about the man. Fantasized about him for months now. It still boggled her brain that he was real. But he was so much more than the writer had been able to portray in the book.

He was a living, breathing, sensual man in his prime. Older than he'd been depicted but more handsome than her imagination had been able to conjure. It didn't matter that he was a virtual stranger. He didn't feel like one. It was if she'd always known him.

She trusted him and that was the most bizarre feat of all. For she'd trusted very few people in her lifetime, never knowing who might be spies for her father. Tienan and Logan were the only other people in her life that she had trusted before Marc.

He sat on his knees by the side of the tub, watching her. Waiting. The surety that he would walk away if she asked him to struck her like a bolt of lightning. He truly meant it when he said she was in charge. A thrilling sense of feminine power shot through her at the thought of being in control of all that masculine sexuality. Her nipples tightened and heat pooled between her thighs.

She nodded slowly and Marc's posture relaxed, revealing exactly how tense he'd been. He stripped off his vest, leaving his chest bare. She'd seen it before but she hadn't taken the time to really look at it.

The light from the candles flickered, bathing his skin, giving it a golden glow. The man was built. She was used to the lean, supple muscles of Tienan and Logan. Marc was very different. His shoulders were incredibly wide and thick, his biceps huge. The metal arm and wristbands only emphasized their size and strength. A light sprinkling of hair dusted the center of his chest and tapered down his belly. Muscles banded his stomach. His waist was thick but there wasn't an ounce of fat on the man.

From her vantage point in the tub, she couldn't see much below his waist, although she knew what was below it was as impressive as what was above. She'd seen his erection and the heated glint in his eyes. There was no doubt that he wanted her.

For a woman who'd always been treated as an oddball, a misfit, this was heady stuff. There was no faking that kind of response and it was an aphrodisiac to be wanted so much by a man like this.

She sucked in a breath when he leaned across her and plucked the bar of soap off the shelf. "I'll wash your hair first." He positioned himself behind her. She could hear the sound of his breathing but she couldn't see him.

She felt nervous and excited all at once. Her earlier sleepiness had fled, replaced by a rush of adrenaline and anticipation. His fingers sifted through her hair, plucking out the few remaining pins. They plinked against the stone floor as he dropped them. His motions were firm and sure as he messaged her scalp for a moment before sliding his fingers through the tresses to loosen any tangles.

"Lie back," he murmured.

Falling under his seductive spell, she slid downward in the tub until her hair was immersed in the water. When it was totally soaked, she sat up and he began to work. He wrapped his arms around her, dipped the soap in the water and worked a thick lather between his palms. Laying the soap on her tummy, he then proceeded to work the lather through her hair from root to tip. He worked slowly and methodically. Kathryn felt the stress of the day slip away.

Closing her eyes, she was lost to his tender ministrations. "Back down," he instructed. Without opening her eyes, she submerged totally beneath the water. She felt his hands in her hair, working the soap out. She sat back up, sputtering when she could no longer hold her breath.

Marc handed her a cloth and she swiped her face. "Thanks."

"I'm going to give it a final rise." He stood and picked up a bucket from the far side of the tub. "Tip your head back."

Kathryn scooted forward and did as he asked. Carefully, he poured the clean water over her scalp and hair. When he was done, he gently twisted the mass, wringing the water from it. She couldn't believe how much better she felt simply having her hair clean.

"Now I can bathe you."

She shivered but not because she was cold. Her blood pumped heavily through her veins as heat suffused every inch of her. She felt alive for the first time in her life. It was as if every cell in her body was poised, ready for what was to come.

"Yes," she sighed and sat back, taking care to drape the bulk of her hair over the rim of the tub so it didn't trail into the water.

Reaching down, he dug around the tub until he found the bar of soap and lathered his hands once again. This time, he placed them on the curve of her neck and stroked up and down the slender column. She tilted her head back, peeking out from under her lids to study him.

His face was wreathed in concentration as he worked. With great deliberation, he soaped her shoulders and arms. Then, one hand at a time, he carefully washed the bloodstains from all her fingers.

She decided that she could easily watch him for hours. His face was so masculine, almost hard. He had a high forehead and cheekbones and full lips. His golden-brown eyes reminded her of an eagle that she'd seen in a picture book when she was a child. The species was extinct on earth but once it had been one of the fiercest birds of prey on the planet. Marc was like that—fierce, ready to attack at a moments notice. But there was another side to him as well. A gentle side. The side he was showing her now.

His hands shifted, slipping over the mounds of her breasts. A whimper of pleasure escaped her as he tenderly plucked at her nipples. The electric sensation seemed to shoot from her breasts to her pussy. Her inner muscles contracted and relaxed. She felt empty. Needy. Her hips undulated in the water, sending a wave of water to the edge of the tub.

"More?" Marc asked as he slid his hands over her tummy.

"Yes." She parted her legs and arched her hips. She wanted, no needed, him to touch her. To sate the ache within her, which went all the way to the very core of her being. "Touch me." She didn't recognize her own voice. Gone was the sharp, crisp tone she usually used, replaced by a sultry whisper that invited and beguiled.

Marc traced her belly button, dipping a finger inside before continuing his journey. He cupped her hips in his hands, his thumbs brushing her hipbones. She giggled at the unexpected touch. His fingers tickled her skin and she squirmed beneath his hands.

"Ah," he breathed. "You're ticklish."

"I'm not," she gasped, trying not to laugh.

Marc's low chuckle filled the air. "I'll have to remember that."

Without warning, he slid between her legs, holding the slick folds of her sex open with one hand, while plunging two fingers deep inside her. The juxtaposition from laughter to carnal delight had her head spinning and her emotions shattered. She had no defenses against Marc. Nor did she want any. Not now. Maybe in the bright light of the morning, but for now, she just wanted to feel.

Kathryn cried out, arching her hips. She felt stretched. Full. It was delicious. As in her dream, it barely took a touch and she was close to climax. Never in her life had she felt so sexually charged and sensually alive.

"You're so tight," he gritted out. "So hot." He slid his fingers to the edge of her opening.

She shoved her hips upward, not wanting to lose contact with him. She bit her lip to keep from screaming in frustration when he fingered the folds of her sex. Reaching down, she grabbed his hand and pushed it lower.

"Tell me what you want?"

"You," she gasped as his thumb stroked her swollen clit. "Your fingers inside me, fucking me." She'd never talked like this in her life but she was desperate. She wanted this. Needed this release.

"Whatever you want, Kathryn. If it is within my power to give it, it is yours." One thick finger slid into her tight sheath. When he withdrew to the edge, he pushed a second one inside. The water, her arousal and the soap on his fingers allowed them to slide easily. His rhythm quickened as he drove her higher and higher.

Energy coiled low in her belly. She was so close. Her breathing was ragged as she grasped the edge of the tub and met the inward stroke of his fingers with a thrust of her hips. She tilted her head back, her mouth parting on a low cry.

"More," she screamed.

Marc brushed his thumb against her clit as he pumped his fingers. Leaning down, he nuzzled her neck before gently biting. Her fingers tingled, her nipples tightened and her entire body jerked. Kathryn cried his name as she came. Water sloshed as she pumped her hips, desperate to milk every last sensation from her climax.

When she could take no more, she clamped her thighs together. Marc carefully withdrew his fingers and buried his face in her neck. His breathing was as heavy as hers as they both sat there. Kathryn shivered, a combination of the remnants of her climax and the cool air. The water had chilled and she was cold now that the heat of the moment had passed.

Marc moved around to the side of the tub. Grabbing the soap, he quickly washed her legs and feet before dragging a washcloth over her torso. Tossing the cloth aside, he leaned in and scooped her from the tub.

Standing her on the floor, he quickly toweled her off and squeezed the excess water from her hair. He tossed the towel aside and pulled her into his arms once again, carrying her from the bathing chamber and back into the bedroom.

Kathryn tried to look around but the room was in shadows. The cheery fire crackling in the grate, the only light. She felt exhausted, yet energized. It was an odd feeling. Almost one of anticipation.

Marc didn't carry her to the bed. Instead, he laid her atop a thick fur on the floor in front of the fireplace. The warmth from the fire stroked over her skin, warming her. As she watched, he shucked his boots and removed the arm and wristbands, laying them carefully on the mantle. His hands went to the laces at the front of his pants.

Her eyes traced the long, thick bulge and she felt cream slip from her pussy. She wanted him. And this time, she wanted his thick, hard length inside her, filling her.

He quickly loosened the laces and shoved his pants over his muscular legs and off. She made a low humming sound in the back of her throat. She'd never seen anything like him in her life. She longed to touch him, to taste him.

She licked her lips and he groaned. Her gaze shot to his face and she saw lust and longing etched there. Holding out her hand, she beckoned to him. "Come here."

Chapter Six
છ

Marc gritted his teeth and braced his muscles to keep from falling on Kathryn and rutting like a bull scenting a female in season. Her skin glowed in the flickering light, the damp tresses of her hair gleamed. When it was dry, he knew her hair would rival the fire itself. He'd never seen hair quite that color. It was vibrant and alive. Just like her.

Standing beside her, he gazed down. The dream didn't do her justice. Marc wasn't sure how much had been a dream and how much had been real but it no longer mattered. She was here now and he was going to do everything in his power to keep her.

She swallowed and he watched the slender column of her neck ripple. He shuddered as a rush of arousal shot through him. His cock was fully aroused. Hard and long, it jerked slightly as if trying to reach for her.

Marc went down on his knees beside her. "Turn around so your back is toward the flames." He waited until she was settled, then he carefully spread the long cape of her hair toward the heat. "I don't want you to get sick," he murmured as he combed his fingers through her thick tresses.

"That feels wonderful," she sighed. Closing her eyes, she tilted her head slightly, relaxing into his caress.

He smiled. How like a contented cat she looked, all but purring as he stroked her. As her hair dried, he could see the brilliant reddish tones more clearly. Strands curled slightly around his fingers as he continued to work carefully. There were a few tangles but he patiently got rid of them one at a time.

When he was satisfied that she was dry and warm, he shifted, stretching out beside her. Kathryn smiled sleepily as she rolled onto her back. "Thank you."

"My pleasure." The words were little more than a deep rumble. In truth, he was finding it hard to talk. His entire body was on fire with need for her. Yet, he wasn't ready to take her. Not yet. First he wanted to touch her. To explore the bounty laid bare before him.

Supporting himself on one arm, he cupped her chin in his hand, rubbing his thumb over her smooth cheek. Her skin was softer than the finest furs. He leaned closer, studying her. One by one he touched the few freckles that dotted her otherwise pale skin.

She wrinkled her nose slightly. "I've never liked my freckles."

"Why?" How could she not like them? He found them fascinating.

"They make me look like a kid."

He chuckled. "That is not possible, Kathryn. Believe me. There is no doubt that you are all woman."

She blinked as he stroked his thumb over the curve of her bottom lip. Her mouth parted slightly and he pushed the tip of his thumb inside. Kathryn moaned sexily and nipped the edge of his skin. Now it was his turn to groan.

Her tongue slid over the top of his thumb and down the sides. Marc couldn't stand it any longer. Pulling his thumb away, he leaned down and tasted her lips. It was the barest of touches but it made his head spin. She smelled of soap and flowers and a hint of womanly musk. She tasted of promises and tomorrows.

Her lips parted as he stroked his tongue inside. Lazily, he explored the wet cavern, tangling his tongue with hers in a slow mating dance. Her hands slid up his biceps, her short nails lightly scoring his skin. His body felt alive with anticipation. With longing.

The kiss went on and on. Marc slid his hand around to the back of her head, cupping her skull with his palm, holding her captive as he plundered her mouth. Her hands slid up his shoulders and neck before she buried them in his hair. Her fingertips massaged his scalp. The sensation was incredible and he let out a deep rumble of pleasure.

Kathryn's legs moved restlessly against his. He broke the kiss and stared into her deep green eyes. A man could willingly lose himself in such eyes. He touched her lips one final time and then peppered her forehead, cheeks and nose with kisses, making sure his lips touched each freckle.

He worked his way down the curve of her neck to her shoulders, all the while ignoring the ache in his cock. It throbbed in time to his heartbeat and liquid seeped from the tip. His balls were heavy and full, the skin pulled so tight around them it was a wonder they didn't burst. He'd never felt need like this in his life. It gnawed at his belly like a savage hunger and ate at his soul.

Yet, he wanted her pleasure before his own.

Her collarbone seemed incredibly fragile beneath his fingers. Once again he was reminded of how much smaller than he she was. Her personality was so vibrant and alive, she projected the image of someone larger. Not that she was short, because she wasn't, but she was slender and delicate.

She tightened her fingers in his hair and tugged his head lower. He couldn't suppress the smile that formed on his lips. Delicate she might be but she wasn't shy about letting him know what she wanted.

His lips found the curve of her breast and he licked her soft, slightly salty skin. "Marc." His skin rippled with arousal as she longingly whispered his name. He plumped her breast in his hand and curled his tongue around her nipple. It was pink and puckered and tasted sweet.

She moaned, her fingers digging into his scalp as she tugged him closer. Parting his lips, he tugged her turgid nipple into his mouth and sucked. She shifted beneath him, her hips moving restlessly. He could feel her heart pounding in her chest.

Need was building rapidly within him and he knew he was running out of time. Giving her nipple one final suck, he released it and quickly moved down her torso, kissing and licking a path down her rib cage to her belly. Her stomach was flat, emphasizing her hipbones. He placed a tender kiss on each one, the urge to feed her, to take care of her, riding him hard. But first he had to claim her. Mark her as his.

Settling on his stomach between her legs, he placed a hand on each thigh and pushed her legs wider, exposing her soft, wet cunt. She made a soft sound but didn't protest.

"You are so beautiful." His words were slow, his tongue felt thick in his mouth. "So pink and wet. You're glistening with need." He stroked a finger over the slick folds. As he watched, cream slipped from her core. "And it's all for me, isn't it, Kathryn?"

"Yes," she moaned, tilting her hips toward him.

Satisfaction roared through him and his cock jerked. Swearing under his breath, he pressed his cock against the fur, trying to keep from spilling his seed right then and there. Blood pounded in his veins, all of it flowing to the engorged shaft between his thighs.

He inhaled deeply, drawing her unique fragrance into his lungs. The scent of Kathryn's arousal was intoxicating. Moving closer, he lapped at her sensitive flesh with his tongue, tasting her essence. He moaned when it touched his lips and tongue. This was better than any dream. This was pure pleasure.

Her hips swiveled and jerked as he stroked over her thick folds, teasing the bundle of nerves at the apex of her thighs. "Marc," she gasped.

He captured her clitoris between his lips and sucked gently. She cried out, thrashing her head from side to side. He released the tender bud and blew softly. "What?"

She gave a strangled laugh. "You beast. You know what I want."

"Tell me." He pushed the tip of his index finger barely inside her sheath, rimming it.

Planting her feet on the rug, she pushed her hips upward, taking his finger deeper into her heated passage. "You," she panted, her chest rising and falling rapidly. "I want you."

Marc looked up from between her spread thighs, admiring the erotic picture she made sprawled across the thick, dark fur. Her breasts swayed with every breath she took, her nipples were tight and deeper in color. Her skin appeared flushed as blood pumped quickly through her veins. Her eyes were half closed, her lips parted.

He pushed his finger as far as it would go and slowly withdrew it, curving it upward as he did so. Kathryn gasped and he felt her inner muscles flutter and tighten around him. "You want me?"

"Yes."

"You want me to fuck you?" Her sheath tightened and more of her essence coated his finger as he pushed it inward once again. "Say the words." He needed her to say them. Had to hear them from her sweet lips.

"Fuck me," she groaned.

"Say my name." He pushed a second finger inside her, spreading them apart, widening her.

Her hips jerked and a low scream came from deep in her throat. She squeezed his fingers tightly, her muscles rippling as she came. He got what he wanted though. As she shuddered through her orgasm, his name fell from her lips.

"Marc," she cried out as orgasm overtook her. Her body clutched at his fingers and she felt the dampness between her thighs. *Twice*! was all she could think. This is the second orgasm within about a half hour. Amazing.

Then she couldn't think at all. When she finally came back to herself, she looked down, shuddering at the erotic vision.

Her nipples were hard buds, so flushed they appeared red. Her skin glistened with a light sheen of perspiration. She was no longer cold, that's for sure. Her legs were sprawled wide and Marc's head rested on her belly, his long brown hair falling across her thigh and down her hip as his fingers gently played with her slick folds, more soothing than arousing. His eyes were closed and the corners of his mouth were tilted in a slight smile.

Her core pulsed and although she'd come twice, satisfaction eluded her. She needed more. She needed Marc.

When she shifted, he lifted his head, slowly rising, to sit on his heels. Kathryn bit her lip to keep from crying out as a lock of his waist-length hair brushed over her pussy. She was incredibly sensitive. Amazingly enough, merely looking at him was enough to start her body humming again.

She loved his face. He wasn't handsome in a classic sense but his features were strong and blunt and masculine. His shoulders and chest were impossibly wide and firm. His abdomen a sculpted work of art.

And jutting out from a nest of dark hair was a very impressive erection. His shaft was thick and long, the network of blue veins pulsing heavily. The cock head was dark, engorged with blood and pre-cum oozed from the tip. She licked her lips and Marc groaned.

Her gaze flew to his and she realized he was watching her every move. She was filled with the urge to give him the kind of pleasure that he'd given to her. Slowly, she came up on her knees. The soft fur was a sensual caress against her skin.

Never in her life has she felt so sexually alive and so aware of every inch of her own flesh as well as his. It was as if all her senses were heightened. Every nerve ending in her body twitched and quivered as she moved toward him. His face hardened, his hands fisted at his sides.

Feminine power rushed through her as she realized that she affected him the same way he did her. Oh, this was marvelous, empowering and an incredible aphrodisiac. Placing her hands on his knees, she skimmed her fingers upward to the tops of his thighs. The wiry hair on his thighs brushed against her palms, making her hands tingle.

The fire crackled beside her and she could hear a slight wind outside the window but other than that there was only the sound of their breathing. The thick stone walls shut out all other sounds, cocooning them in this erotic space and time.

Kathryn no longer felt like her normal, dull, conservative self. She felt alive and filled with power, need and longing. Gone was the feeling of awkwardness she usually had around the opposite sex. For some reason it felt perfectly natural to be totally naked in front of Marc.

Tomorrow she might feel differently but for tonight, she wanted to celebrate life. She, Tienan and Logan had somehow made it out of their desperate situation alive. Tienan had survived her primitive surgery and would no doubt recover. And Marc, the man she'd fantasized and spun erotic dreams around for months, was right in front of her, waiting for her to touch him.

She would deal with reality tomorrow. Tonight was for her. For them.

Tentatively, she cupped the heavy sac between his thighs, squeezing gently. "Kathryn." He gritted out her name from between clenched teeth. Sweat popped out on his forehead. She realized that he was close to coming.

"Hmmm," she answered, which was really no answer at all. She had to touch him, to taste him. Leaning forward, she delicately licked at the slit at the tip of his erection. He tasted salty and musky. She wanted more.

Slowly, she curled her tongue around the head of his cock, taking care to trace the ridge. His hips jerked and she tasted more of his arousal on her lips. She licked them and shuddered. The throbbing between her thighs intensified. Her breasts ached.

Grabbing his hands, she pressed them against her. He sucked in a deep breath as he uncurled his fingers and cupped the plump mounds. She could feel the tight buds pressing into the center of his palms.

She started to lower her head again but he stopped her. "No more. I'm too close." She peered up at him, noting the heat in his eyes, the flush on his skin.

Kathryn felt brazen and wanton. "Take me then."

His eyes narrowed, his lips firmed. "Turn over on your hands and knees. I want to take you from behind."

Her heart jumped and began to beat rapidly. She'd never had a man do that to her before. She bit her bottom lip. Part of her wanted this but another part was afraid. She didn't really know Marc at all, did she?

As if sensing her growing unease, he soothed her bottom lip with his thumb as he leaned down and kissed her. "I will never hurt you, Kathryn. All you have to do is say the words and we'll stop."

She paused and stared at him. He was totally serious. She'd never met a man like him before. She was naked before him and he'd already given her two spectacular orgasms. He was also naked and so close to coming, yet he was willing to walk away if that was what she wanted.

All her doubts fled. This was a man she could trust with her body, with her very life. Indeed, he'd already saved her life. Leaning forward, she kissed him softly, their lips barely touching. "Thank you." He nodded and lowered his head, taking several deep breaths.

She shifted, turning so her hands and knees supported her. When he didn't move, she glanced over her shoulder. He hadn't budged, his head was still down and he was breathing slowly. He thought she was saying no to him.

"Marc."

Very slowly he lifted his head. Lust blazed from his eyes. They widened and then narrowed as he took in her position. "Are you sure?"

Her heart skipped a beat. Even now he was giving her a choice. "Yes." She leaned forward, tilting her backside upward.

Groaning, Marc positioned himself between her legs, pushing them wider. Kathryn let her head fall forward, savoring the feel of his hair-roughened thighs against hers. His shaft stroked over her swollen flesh and she sucked in a breath as he pulled back and positioned the head of his cock at her opening. He pressed barely inside, stretching her channel to accommodate him.

He began to move slowly, pulling back and pushing forward an inch at a time. Her inner muscles stretched and clenched, adjusting to his girth as he worked deeper. It was heaven. It was torture. She wanted him all the way inside her. Now. But she also knew his way was best. It had been a long time since she'd made love and never with a man of his size.

Marc reached around her, cupping her breasts as his hips began to pump harder. He filled her now. She felt full and stretched and wonderful. He angled her hips so his balls slapped against her clit with each thrust. She gasped and shoved her hips back to meet each of his strokes.

His fingers plied her nipples, pinching and soothing them at turns. Nothing else existed to Kathryn except reaching fulfillment. The soft furs ticked her hands and knees as Marc's hands cupped her breast and squeezed. He released one mound and slid his hand lower, toward her belly. She gasped, contracting her inner muscles tight around him as his finger slid through her pubic hair, finding her clit.

"Harder," she gasped.

She felt his lips on her spine, nipping and sucking. "Your pussy is so hot and tight around my cock." His erotic words

77

made her heart skip a beat. Her core tightened around him and he gave a strangled laugh.

"Just like that," he encouraged her. "Squeeze my cock again. I want to feel the walls of your cunt wrapped tight around every inch." He pulled back and thrust forward. Harder this time. "You want it hard?"

"God yes," she moaned as a lock of his long hair brushed against her side. Using her hands for leverage, she shoved against him on every forward stroke.

Marc grabbed her hips and began to pump heavily, pounding into her body. She could feel the orgasm gathering deep in her core. Throwing her head back, she cried out as he surged heavily within her. Every cell in her body seemed to explode, hips jerking wildly as she came.

She heard him call her name and felt the flood of heat as he spent himself within her. Her pussy tightened and fluttered as she continued to orgasm. Her entire body quivered and finally, her hands and knees gave out and she collapsed onto the fur rug.

Marc's cock slipped from her and she cried out at the loss. He wrapped his arms around her, covering her legs and back with his body. Kathryn had no idea how long they'd been lying there when Marc finally moved. She thought about getting up and crawling into bed but it seemed like too much trouble.

A few seconds later, Marc was back and pressing a damp cloth between her legs. She buried her face against the fur, feeling the heat in her cheeks. It was ridiculous to be embarrassed at this point but she couldn't help it. Without the heat of passion driving her onward, she reverted back to her shy, quiet self.

Marc finished cleaning her and tossed the cloth aside before rolling her onto her back. She tried to open her eyes but yawned instead. Her mouth opened so wide her jaw made a little popping sound. Strong arms lifted her and carried her across the room. She sighed when she felt the mattress beneath her. Suddenly, she was beyond exhausted. She was so tired she wasn't even hungry anymore.

The mattress dipped and Marc gathered her into his arms. "Sleep." He pressed a kiss on her forehead and she sighed, throwing her arm across him. "We'll talk tomorrow."

That sounded ominous but she didn't care. All she wanted to do right now was sleep.

* * * * *

Jarek was leaning on the wall just beyond the door when Marc let himself out of Kathryn's room. "How is she?"

Marc made sure the door was closed before answering. "She's fine. Sleeping."

His brother met his gaze, his eyes as serious as Marc had ever seen them. "You've already claimed her."

It was not a question, but Marc nodded.

"This is unprecedented." Jarek fingered the pommel of the sword strapped to his side. "There will be repercussions."

"I know." And he did. What he wanted was against all the laws of their people.

"By law, although I am Christina's husband, you are legally bound to her and yet you have taken another woman."

"I renounce all claim to Christina, now and forever."

Jarek's body jerked as though he'd been physically struck. "No one has ever done such a thing in the history of our world."

"I have no choice." Marc sighed, raking his fingers through his hair. "Our relationship has been in name only for a long time now. It is not a true joining as most marriages in our world are and we all know it."

Jarek started to speak, but Marc held up his hand. "It is no one's fault, but it is the truth. Try as she might, Christina wants only you in her bed." He tried to find a way to make his brother understand just what Kathryn meant to him. "The tapestry took me to her."

"You disappeared so suddenly. I did not think I would ever see you again." Marc heard it then, the fear in his brother's voice.

"I had no choice and would do it again in a heartbeat." Marc rubbed his hand over his chest, feeling the heavy throb of his heart beneath his palm. "Kathryn is mine. I would die to protect her."

"You will not be able to keep her for yourself." Jarek reached out to Marc, but let his hand drop as his brother took a step back. "There are laws. People will protest."

"I saved her life back in her world. There are men there who want her dead, who want all three of them dead. The tapestry brought them all here. There is a reason for that." Marc allowed his fear to show for the first time.

"Perhaps that reason is so she can be a bride to another family?" Jarek gently interjected.

"No." Marc's voice was a tortured whisper. "There is a way around this. I know there is. There has to be."

His older brother reached out his arm and clasped his shoulder. Muttering an oath, Jarek pulled him into his arms. "I will stand beside you," Jarek promised. "No matter what comes, I will stand with you."

Marc blinked as his brother released him, overcome by emotion. "Thank you." His brother hadn't needed to say it. Marc never doubted for a moment that his brother would stand behind him in the troubles ahead.

"Christina is waiting to talk to you." Jarek motioned him up the hall with a jerk of his head.

Marc sighed, knowing he had to have this discussion sooner or later and he'd rather have it done with. Following his brother, Marc felt the pull of Kathryn with every step he took away from her. It was only the knowledge that she was safe and would be there in the morning that allowed him to keep going.

Chapter Seven

ဢ

Kathryn woke slowly. She'd had the strangest dreams. Some of them had been more like nightmares. She shuddered and buried her face against her pillow. The General and her father had discovered what she'd done. She'd raced home but not in time to save Tienan and Logan. There had been shooting and Tienan had been wounded.

She shivered, bringing the covers closer to her face. She wrinkled her nose as the fabric stroked her face. It felt unusual, not like her heavy cotton comforter. She stilled as more memories crowded her brain. Had she really performed surgery to remove the bullet from Tienan's shoulder?

She carefully opened one eye and then slammed it shut. This couldn't be happening. It was real. All of it. That meant that she'd spent the night engaging in the most wicked sex of her life with a man who was little more than a stranger. The problem was that Marc didn't feel like a stranger. Being with him had felt right and natural.

Her stomach growled, reminding her vividly that she hadn't eaten since breakfast yesterday and not much even then. Forcing herself to open her eyes, she pushed up and glanced around. Sunshine was streaming in through the two tall, thin windows. They were both made of vibrant stained glass and the colors flashed on the stone walls and floor. It seemed that she'd slept most of the morning away.

The covering dipped low and she grabbed it back to her chest. She was naked and had no idea where her clothing was. Not that she had a top to wear. Her blouse had been sacrificed yesterday. But a bra and dirty pants was better than running around naked.

Sliding her feet over the side of the bed, she let them hit the floor, tugging the thick fur with her. She wrapped it around her, tucking in the ends to create a sarong dress of sorts. The bed she'd been sleeping in was huge with four large posts, one on each corner. Bed curtains hung on thin rails that ran from post to post. She imagined they would be cozy on a cold night.

The room itself was sparse but the furniture that was here looked inviting. A low bench sat in front of one of the windows, inviting a person to sit and peer out at the land beyond. A trunk sat at the end of the bed, a place for storage and another makeshift seat. Two chairs were angled in front of the fireplace, a low wooden table between them.

What was on the table caught her eye immediately. Food. Her stomach growled loudly and she scooted forward, curling her toes against the cool stone beneath her feet. She felt her cheeks heating when she stepped onto the fur rug that lay in front of the fireplace. What she and Marc had done there last night… She fanned her face as she examined the food.

There was a jug of clear water and one of what smelled like apple cider. Licking her lips, she poured some of the water into a wooden cup and drank it all down. Then she did it again. Thirst quenched, she poured a glass of the cider and sipped as she examined the food. There was a thick loaf of dark, crusty bread, some pale yellow cheese, some apples and what appeared to be some sort of cold meat. Ignoring the meat, she broke off a section of bread and slapped a piece of the cheese on it. Biting off a corner, she began to chew.

Flavor exploded in her mouth. This was good. She munched happily, taking the occasional sip of the cider as she ordered her thoughts. She had no idea where Marc was or when he'd left her. Part of her was glad for a few moments to herself but another part of her was disappointed he hadn't been beside her when she woke.

Finishing off the slice of bread and cheese, she licked her fingers and stared longingly at the table. She'd take another slice with her. Right now, she needed to find her clothing and to check on Tienan and Logan. Then they needed to figure out what the heck they were going to do about their situation. If the information in the book was correct, the tapestry should reappear sometime tomorrow to take them home.

Taking a final sip of the sweet cider, she put the glass aside and padded toward the door in the corner. She hoped her clothing was still in the bathing room. The tub was empty but there was a basin of water on a stand in the corner and the water was still warm. Dropping her fur, she washed and dried her body quickly, using the soap and cloth she found next to the basin.

Her bra and panties were draped across a wooden rod. They were damp to the touch but not too bad. Someone had obviously washed them and hung them to dry. She wasn't sure she liked the idea of some stranger touching her underwear but she was too glad for clean clothing to worry about it. She slipped them on, shivering slightly at the cold dampness. It was better than running around half naked.

Her shoes were there but her socks were missing. There was also no sign of her pants but there was a robe on a hook by the door. She slipped it on. The dark green fabric was soft against her skin but the hem pooled around her feet. It was obviously meant for a much taller and bigger person. Marc?

She ignored the warm glow that started low in her stomach as she knotted the belt around her waist. It would do for now. She thought about slipping on her shoes but didn't want to wear them without her socks. Glancing around, she found a wooden comb and worked the tangles out of her hair before braiding it. She looked around for something to tie the ends but came up empty handed.

Shuffling back to the bedroom, she figured she'd look there. Maybe there was something in the trunk that would do. The first thing she noticed was her purse tucked away by the head of the bed. She'd missed it when she'd rolled out of bed. Hurrying forward, she picked it up, upending everything onto the bed. Several elastics tumbled out and she grabbed one and twisted it around the end of her hair to hold her braid together.

Her sewing kit and small makeup bag were there, along with her wallet, a pack of tissues, her key cards, work ID card, a half eaten chocolate bar and some loose change. Unzipping the makeup bag, she ignored the tweezers, which had been cleaned, and pulled out her small bottle of moisturizer and her lip balm. That was the extent of her makeup.

Pouring some of the lotion onto her fingers, she rubbed it over her face before capping the bottle and shoving everything back into her bag. Nothing there for her to wear. Tucking the bag back where she'd found it, she then went to the trunk at the end of the bed and opened it. She'd barely started rummaging around when a knock came on the door.

Holding the lapels of the robe together, she walked slowly to the door. "Yes?"

The handle turned and the door opened and Christina stuck her head in through the opening. "Are you up for a visitor?"

Kathryn knew she had to deal with the reality of the situation. Seemed as if her reprieve was over. Besides, she was interested in the woman who'd left her life behind to stay and make a life in this strange world. "Come in."

Christina entered, closing the door behind her. She was wearing a floor-length blue dress that matched her eyes. In her hands, she had a bundle of clothing, which she offered to Kathryn. "I figured you'd be looking for something to wear right about now."

"Thank you." Gratitude flowed through her. "I couldn't find my pants this morning and my blouse is a total write-off." And she was babbling because she was nervous.

It suddenly occurred to her that she'd slept with a man who was emotionally and physically tied to this woman. Marc might not be Christina's husband, but they had been intimate. Very intimate.

Her stomach was suddenly queasy and the food she'd eaten threatened to come back up. She'd slept with another woman's man! When it was happening, it had felt so natural and right that she hadn't even questioned it. In her mind, Marc was hers.

What had she done? Maybe Christina didn't know what had happened between her and Marc last night. Not that it made the situation any better, but Kathryn didn't want to hurt the other woman.

To hide her trepidation, she started to sort through the garments, stopping when she found a pair of loose trousers.

"I thought you'd like those." Christina smiled but Kathryn could see the strain around her eyes and mouth.

"I'm sorry if we've brought trouble to your home." She could only imagine how the other woman must have felt with three complete strangers invading her home, delivered by a magical tapestry, no less.

Christina shook her head, making her long, white-blonde hair shimmer. "It's not that." She walked over to the bed and sat on the end as Kathryn tugged on the pants. They were a bit large but there was a drawstring belt, which tightened nicely.

"What then?" Kathryn paused, pants on and robe open.

"Javara is different…" Christina trailed off, as if not quite sure what to say next.

Kathryn wrapped her arms around herself, rubbing her hands over her suddenly chilled flesh. "Women here are scarce and brothers compete sexually for a woman. She can only marry one but she has relations with the other. You chose Jarek but Marc feels left out."

Christina looked as if all the blood had drained from her face, she was so pale. "How…how do you know?"

"So, I'm right?"

Threads of Destiny

Christina nodded.

Sighing, Kathryn rubbed her temples. She had the beginnings of one heck of a tension headache brewing. "I read it in a book."

Christina's mouth dropped open. "A book?"

"Yeah. It was written about a hundred years before my time. I found it in the attic in my family home and read it."

"That's impossible."

Kathryn gave the other woman a wry smile. "That's what I'm thinking about all of this."

"What did the book say?" Christina bit her bottom lip, her cheeks turning a bright shade of red.

"Ah…" she began and then broke off. How did you tell a woman that her entire sex life had been put down on paper? "It was pretty explicit."

Christina buried her face in her hands, her shoulders shaking. Kathryn didn't know what to do. How did you comfort a woman at a time like this? When the other woman raised her head, tears rolled down her cheeks. But she was laughing.

"Oh my God," she gasped. "I had such a boring life back on Earth before the tapestry came. Whoever would have thought I'd be the subject of a book. How?"

Kathryn grinned, glad to see that Christina seemed to be taking it so well. "I have no idea. All I know is that a book exists and it tells all about your journey to Javara and the sexual exploits that ensued. I particularly liked the scene with you and Jarek on the horse."

Christina's jaw dropped and then she began to laugh again, swiping at the tears on her cheeks with the back of her hand. "This is unbelievable."

"It was quite educational, I assure you," she added dryly, before joining in the laughter. Christina's sense of humor was infectious. Rather than being upset, as most women would be, she was finding the humor in the situation.

In spite of everything, Kathryn found herself liking Christina. And that made her feel doubly guilty about what she and Marc had done last night.

"What was the book called?"

"Christina's Tapestry. It's actually quite a beautiful book. I cried near the end when I thought you were leaving."

"Imagine that." Shaking her head, Christina pinned Kathryn with her pale blue eyes. "What year do you come from? You said you thought we were from much different times."

"If the book is correct, and it seems to be accurate so far, then we're a little over one hundred years apart. It was 2133 when we left. September to be accurate."

Christina's mouth was wide open and she closed it abruptly. "I don't know why I'm so shocked. I mean the tapestry came into my life and brought me here. Why shouldn't it go to other times? It's just so…" She waved her hand around as if searching for the right word.

"Weird," Kathryn offered.

Christina laughed. "Exactly." She sobered, straightening the skirt on her long, fitted dress. "So you know that the tapestry will be back tomorrow night. You'll have to decide if you're staying or going."

"I'm going."

Christina's eyes widened. "I thought that after last night…" she glanced at the tangle of bedclothes behind her.

Kathryn felt embarrassed to the tips of her toes. So Christina did know what had happened last night. "That was an aberration. I mean, I know that Marc is technically yours, even though he isn't your husband." God, she hadn't even thought about that last night and the guilt was overwhelming her. As far as she was concerned, Marc was a free agent but that wasn't quite how things worked here.

"No, Marc is not mine. Not anymore. I'm not sure he ever was," she sighed. "He hasn't been with me in over a year. He's pulled away from us because he knows that I love Jarek." Christina rose and began to pace. "I tried to embrace the customs of this world but it felt strange. I mean, I love Marc but not in the way I love Jarek."

Kathryn nodded, not quite knowing what to say.

Sadness emanated from Christina as she continued her restless pacing. "There is no need for you to feel bad about what happened between you and Marc. Our relationship is complicated, but it's not sexual. Not anymore. Marc is a good friend, a brother-in-law."

The other woman seemed so distressed that Kathryn reached out to her. "I understand. You can't just throw off your own background and upbringing." She wanted to do something to help but didn't quite know what to do. She'd never had a female friend before. "Would you like some chocolate?" she offered. "I've got a half a bar and its kinda squashed but you can have it." Now how lame was that.

"Chocolate." The tone of Christina's voice bordered on reverence as she sidled up alongside Kathryn. "You have chocolate?"

"Ah, yes." Going over to her bag, she dug around inside but couldn't find it. Upending it once again, she dumped everything on the bed. The bar tumbled out along with everything else. A small leather-bound book fell out. Kathryn frowned. That hadn't been there a few minutes ago. Picking it up, she gasped as she realized it was the journal she'd found in the attic. She glanced at Christina but the other woman was staring raptly at the candy bar.

"Help yourself." Kathryn casually tucked the book under her purse, not quite sure why she felt the need to hide it but she did.

"I haven't had chocolate in years." Peeling back the wrapper, Christina sank down on the edge of the trunk took a delicate bite and moaned. "Oh God, this is so good. Thank you."

Kathryn laughed. Seemed that some things didn't change over time. "You're welcome." As she dug through the clothing and found a tunic that looked as if it would fit, she dropped the robe and tugged it on. "How is Tienan?" She berated herself for not asking Christina immediately.

The other woman paused and swallowed, her eyes closed in obvious enjoyment. "He's fine. Better than fine actually. Mara is amazed by how well he's doing. He had a slight fever last night and she gave him a few of the aspirin you left." Christina nibbled off another corner of the bar and moaned. Laughing self-consciously, she glanced away. "You must think I'm nuts."

"Hey, if I hadn't had chocolate in…" She stopped. "How many years have you been here?"

"Six," Christina managed between bites.

Kathryn shook her head in amazement. "If I hadn't had chocolate in that long, I'd probably be doing the same thing."

"The only thing that came with me when the tapestry brought me was the nightgown I was wearing."

Kathryn thought about that for a moment. "I had my purse slung around my neck and shoulder." She shrugged. "Maybe that made the difference." She paused as she examined the fit of the tunic. Long-sleeved, it came down to her butt and had two deep pockets. She liked it. The dark brown looked good. "Although the guns that Tienan and Logan had in their hands disappeared somewhere along the way."

"Maybe it's technology that doesn't travel," Christina surmised. "We have leather and medicine and basic tools here, so maybe that's why your purse made it."

"Guess we'll never know." Reaching under her purse, she pulled out the journal and tucked it in her pocket as Christina munched on the final square of the chocolate. She had to find the time to read it later. She had a feeling it wouldn't have traveled through time if it weren't important. Not for the first time in her life, Kathryn was thankful for the fact that she could speed read and she had a photographic memory.

While Christina finished the last piece of the chocolate, Kathryn strode back into the bathing chamber long enough to grab her shoes. Socks or no socks, she had to wear something on her feet. She pulled them on, grateful that they were flat with rubber souls and laces. They were sturdy and comfortable. Perfect shoes for working in the lab all day. They'd do.

Christina was crumpling the paper when she returned and staring longingly at the wrapper. Giving it one final look, she turned to Kathryn. "If you're ready, I can take you to them." Standing, she wiped her hands together.

The tension was back. There was something the other woman was keeping from her. "What aren't you telling me?"

"I didn't want to tell you this. Not right away." She met Kathryn's gaze squarely. This was so not going to be good. "There is a crowd here at the moment to celebrate the birth of our latest child. A girl—Allina."

"Congratulations." Kathryn knew what a big deal the birth of a girl was here in Javara.

"Thank you. But there are families here. Families with unmated males."

Kathryn took a step back, then stopped. "You mean…" She broke off, not quite sure how to put it.

"They all want you. You're a potential tapestry bride and a healer as well. That makes you doubly valuable in their eyes."

"Of all the archaic bullshit!" She'd barely escaped from one group of maniacs. She didn't want to fall in with another. "Can we just say that Tienan and Logan are my husbands?" They'd fall in with that if she asked them.

Christina shook her head. "Someone already asked Logan if you were married and he said that you weren't. They all know."

"Damn." She'd known that this was a possibility but she'd hoped to avoid it. After all, she only had to get through another two days, less than that really, and she'd be on her way back to her own planet and time.

"There are five families who want to challenge for the right to have you."

"To have me." Anger filled her. It was all fine and good to read about the customs of a land, another thing altogether to experience it firsthand. "I'm not some object to be passed around. A toy that they all want."

"I know." Christina reached out her hand and placed it on Kathryn's shoulder. "You understand how things are here. You know they all honor and respect you."

She shook her head. "How can they? They don't even know me." *Marc knows you,* a little voice in the back of her head spoke up. She shook her head again. "I want to see Tienan and Logan."

"Of course." The other woman looked worried but she said nothing more as she led Kathryn out of the room and down the hall.

Kathryn could feel the weight of the journal in her pocket and hoped she'd find some answers there. Regardless, the tapestry would be back tomorrow night and she, Tienan and Logan would leave. She ignored the pang in her chest at the thought of leaving Marc behind. Maybe he could come with them. The tapestry had allowed him to travel through time and space once before. Why not again? It was something to think about.

Kathryn tucked all such thoughts away as she followed Christina into Tienan's room. Logan was sprawled in a chair, his long legs stretched forward, his hands clasped on his flat stomach. Tienan was lounging on the bed, looking remarkably fit for a man who'd had surgery the day before. You'd never know there was anything wrong with him except for the heavy bandage wrapped around his shoulder. Genetics and his strong will made all the difference in his fast recovery time. Both men jumped to their feet when she entered.

"Are you all right?" Logan wrapped his arms around her, hugging her tightly.

"I'm fine." She buried her face against his chest, seeking his familiar scent. When she pulled away, she offered him a smile. "You?"

"Good." He glanced over at Tienan, who was waiting impatiently. "We passed an uneventful night and have bathed and eaten. Christina made sure we had everything we needed." He offered a smile to the other woman who stood quietly watching them.

It was then she noticed that they were both dressed in the same garb as Marc—leather pants and vests, although neither of them wore armbands. They also wore their own boots.

Tienan's patience was obviously at an end as he dragged her into his arms. She felt his lips against the top of her head. "Thank you," he whispered. She knew he was thanking her for operating on him last night.

"I see you are all up and ready." Marc's tone was hard and cold, his words clipped.

Kathryn jerked away from Tienan's embrace, feeling as if she'd been caught doing something wrong. Which was ridiculous. Tienan and Logan were her friends. Marc was... Well, she wasn't quite sure what he was. Her lover for sure but any more than that was impossible.

He strode forward, looking impossibly large and handsome. His long brown hair was tied back at his nape, making his rough-hewn features appear even more severe. But his golden-brown eyes were warm. No, they were hot as he reached her. His hand snaked around her waist, tugging her from Tienan's embrace and pulling her against his chest.

She knew she should object to such high-handed actions but she couldn't get a word past her lips. Before she could even think of what to say, his head swooped down and he captured her mouth with his.

Heat flooded through her as her body remembered last night. She felt the crotch of her panties getting damp and her breasts swelled. She didn't have to look down to know that her nipples were hard and pressing against the soft cotton tunic she wore. His tongue leisurely claimed hers, twining around it. She moaned slightly, going up on her toes so their bodies were positioned better. His hand slid downward, cupping her ass and pulling her closer. She could feel the hardness of his erection against her mound and tilted her hips inward. The motion rubbed her nipples against his chest, making them ache.

"Ahem." The heavy male voice was tinged with amusement.

Kathryn pulled away, gasping for breath, suddenly aware of the silence around her. Ohmigod, what had she done? And in front of Christina, not to mention Tienan and Logan, no less.

She closed her eyes and sought control. Her hormones were raging totally unrestrained, demanding she find the nearest bed and drag Marc there with her. Heck, they didn't need a bed. They hadn't managed to use one last night and he'd given her three orgasms. And those kinds of thoughts weren't helping her calm down one bit.

Marc slid his hand up her spine, bringing it to rest against the back of her neck. "I trust you slept well."

Oh, there was a wealth of innuendo in his words. She could almost see the testosterone filling the room as he laid claim to her. Why didn't he just scream, *I fucked her last night.* The effect was the same. Kathryn pulled back her foot and kicked him in the shin.

He grunted but didn't even move. Totally pissed off, she drew back her foot again. Before she could kick him, an arm wrapped around her from behind and she was lifted off her feet. Without thinking, she kicked backward, striking Logan in the shin. He had the audacity to laugh at her.

"Put. Me. Down." She said each word slowly. She was beginning to wish she'd never left her room this morning. Maybe she'd go back there and stay until the tapestry came for her.

Logan dropped a kiss on her cheek as he lowered her to her feet. "There's no need to be upset, Kathryn," he whispered in her ear. "You're a beautiful woman. If I'd had you to myself last night, I would have done the same thing that Marc did. I would have claimed you."

Heat rushed through her and not all of it was from embarrassment. She could feel Logan's erection pressing against her back. This was simply too much for her to take in at once. Men had never been interested in her and suddenly she was a femme fatale wanted by two men. She glanced at Tienan and there was no mistaking the heat in his eyes. Okay, make that three.

She rubbed her stomach, which was begging to ache. Maybe she shouldn't have had that cider. Too acidic for her sensitive tummy. If Christina was to be believed, there was a large group of men waiting downstairs as well. It was just too much for her to take in.

"Your stomach is paining again." It was almost an accusation.

She glared at Tienan. "Given the events of this morning, is there any wonder?"

"What is wrong with her stomach? Are you ill?" Marc's arm came around her and his palm settled gently over her tummy.

"It's nothing," she began only to be interrupted by Logan.

"We think it's the start of an ulcer."

Christina stepped forward. "There's some goat's milk in the kitchen and I'm sure that Mara will have some kind of tea that might help."

Logan sent her a grateful smile.

"That's all well and good," she began, feeling the anxiety rising within her once again. "But what about all the men downstairs who want to claim me."

"Over my dead body," three male voices spoke in tandem.

Chapter Eight

℘

Marc kept his eye on Kathryn as he led her down the winding staircase to the great hall below, closely followed by Tienan and Logan. Christina had gone on ahead, giving Kathryn time to compose herself.

He felt anger at himself that he hadn't known about her illness. He should have known. Hadn't he thought she was too thin, like someone who has been sick? Christina had taken him aside and told him exactly what an ulcer was and that the cause was usually stress. He realized then that he had no idea exactly what kind of life she'd come from. What little he'd seen hadn't been good.

He'd staked his claim in front of the other men as soon as he'd walked into the room. Mostly because a bolt of white-hot jealousy had hit him when he'd seen her in another man's arms. These men had a history with her that he did not, a connection that was obvious to anyone who watched them together.

Once again, Marc felt as if he were on the outside looking in.

It hurt when it was his brother and Christina. With Kathryn, he felt a devastating sense of loss. At least he and the other two men were in accord. They would not allow Kathryn to be taken from them. Marc would fight everyone and anyone to keep her with him. They were meant to be. He only needed the time to convince her of that.

Time. Time was the enemy. There was only today and tomorrow left before the tapestry would return and the day was almost half gone already. "Do not be afraid," he whispered. "I will be beside you."

She glanced up at him but said nothing. He wanted to carry her to his room, strip off the trousers and tunic she wore and love her until she screamed with pleasure. Kathryn was an enticing combination of shyness and boldness. One moment she seemed embarrassed that people knew they'd spent the night together, the next she was kicking him in the shins. She was unpredictable and the more he learned about her the more he wanted her.

It had been hard to leave her side this morning. He'd watched her in the early morning sunlight, loving the way her red hair shone. The strands seemed almost alive as he'd gently combed them over his pillow. And soft, ah, her hair was so soft against his cheek. He'd buried his face in the mass and inhaled her unique essence.

His cock had been fully erect and aching from the moment he'd opened his eyes. But he'd seen the dark shadows under her eyes and known that she was unused to late-night sexual activity, on top of everything else that had happened, so he'd left her to sleep. Now, he wished he'd stayed and awakened her properly, licking her soft skin from head to toe before sliding into the moist warmth of her sheath and rocking both of them to completion.

His cock jerked and he swore under his breath. Now was not the time. He discreetly adjusted the bulge in the front of his pants. Luckily, Kathryn didn't seem to notice his discomfort. Even though she was right beside him, she seemed far away at the moment. He knew she was worried about what was to come.

Annoyance ate at him. Did she think he would let them just take her? Didn't she have any faith in his skills?

How could she, he reminded himself. She knew almost nothing of his skill with weapons or in battle. His hand went to the hilt of his sword, his fingers wrapping around it. He glanced over his shoulder and met Tienan's gaze. Both men were now armed with swords as well and Marc had no doubt that they could use them. They handled them with a familiarity that bespoke experience.

The noise below reached up the stairs. All were gathered for the midday meal and for a chance to see Kathryn. She hesitated. Marc paused on the stairs beside her, not wanting to rush her. Squaring her shoulders, Kathryn continued down toward the waiting crowd.

Pride filled him to bursting. With her red hair gleaming, her chin tilted upward and her expression determined, she looked like a queen. "I will lead you to the head table where you will be seated between Jarek and myself. Everyone will know that you are under the protection of the House of Garen."

"Fine. But I plan to set everyone straight about the situation immediately. I am not some object to be fought over and claimed. I am a woman and I make my own choices."

Marc inclined his head, all chance for further conversation gone as they entered the room. As their appearance was noted the voices dropped away until silence reigned. All eyes were on Kathryn and the two men who'd arrived with her. All the unmated men in the room would covet her, while being suspicious of Tienan and Logan.

By now all had heard about their arrival and how Kathryn had performed surgery on Tienan. Her shoulders were set back squarely but her hand shook slightly as they walked toward the head table where Jarek stood waiting with Christina by his side. He squeezed her fingers lightly and was pleased when she returned the gesture.

Mennoc Fairmount stared at her with open lust in his gaze. Marc shot him a glare but it didn't deter the other man. The Dannon and Nardor families, as well as the Forrester and Hunter brothers all looked on with interest. Marc knew they all had unmated brothers who would want the beautiful and skilled woman who walked by his side.

Every muscle in his body tightened in protest and he had to force himself to relax and keep his expression impassive as they finally gained the head of the room. The tapestry had brought him to Kathryn. If she belonged to anyone, it was to him.

Marc seated Kathryn and waited until Christina sat before taking his chair. Logan and Tienan sat to his left, Kathryn to his right. Immediately a voice rang out, breaking the silence. "I challenge for the woman." It was Mennoc Fairmount. The man didn't even have the decency to wait until after Jarek spoke.

Marc began to rise but his brother beat him to it, surging to his feet. As the eldest, it was Jarek's right to speak first but the need to claim Kathryn as his own burned in his gut.

Jarek was wearing the family torque, proclaiming his power and authority to all. "Kathryn Piedmont is a guest of the House of Garen. As such, she is under our protection."

"You already have a woman," another man shouted. Marc's eyes narrowed as he recognized Brand Forrester. There were three Forrester brothers and they had no woman.

"The tapestry has brought her here for a reason," Jarek began, only to be rudely interrupted.

"She was brought here to be a bride to one of us." The four Fairmount brothers all jumped to their feet. Not to be outdone, the Forrester brothers stood and pushed their claim. The Nardor brothers quickly joined in the fray, arguing with the other two families. The two Hunter brothers appeared more amused than anything else, while the Dannon brothers appeared disgusted by the outbreak.

The Bakra brothers sat with their wives and mother, watching the scene unfold. They had already told Jarek that they would support the House of Garen whatever decision they made.

The room was fraught with tension as the arguments mounted. The men's voices rose with each passing second. "She belongs to us!" Mennoc bellowed.

Threads of Destiny

Kathryn was watching it all with wide eyes. Her hands were wrapped tight around the arms of the chair, her knuckles white. Logan and Tienan shifted restlessly beside him. Enough was enough. Marc pushed back his chair and rose to his feet.

Kathryn beat him to it. Jumping up, she grabbed her goblet and flung it at Mennoc's head. The man yelped and jumped back as liquid splashed over his chest. Luckily, the goblet itself missed his head, although not by much. All eyes fell on Kathryn.

"Enough!" she yelled. She stared at them all, disdain in her eyes. "I am not some cow to be bartered over at market."

Mennoc started to speak but she held up her hand to silence him. "You've had your say, now I will have mine." He nodded abruptly and she continued. "You all argue and speak as if your words matter." She rested her hands on the table and Marc could see the fine quivering that shook her arms and shoulders.

"I would not have any of you after this display."

"It does not matter what you want. You are a woman, meant to be a bride to one of us." Marc wanted to hit Enoc Fairmount. Slightly younger than his brother, he had little common sense. Plus, Marc didn't like the way he was staring at Kathryn.

Kathryn shook her head. "I do have a choice. The tapestry brought me here and the tapestry can take me away just as easily." She turned to Jarek and Christina. "Thank you for your hospitality. I'll just wait here until the tapestry returns."

Shouts of denial and dismay erupted. The Forrester brothers turned on the Fairmounts, accusing them of driving Kathryn away. The Nardor brothers began to offer pretty words and compliments to sway her. Marc could have told them it was a waste of their time. Kathryn was not a woman to have her head turned by such things.

"I'm leaving." Kathryn pushed away from the table. Marc fell in beside her, not willing to let her out of his sight. Tienan

101

and Logan were right beside them, arranging themselves so that Kathryn was boxed in on three sides.

The sound of steel being drawn from a scabbard sliced through the arguments. Mennoc Fairmount and his brother Enoc stepped in front of Kathryn, swords drawn. Marc's sword was in his hand before he actually thought about drawing it. Positioning himself in front of Kathryn, he faced down the brothers.

"Stand aside, Garen, you have a woman. Your brother has a wife."

The words were painful daggers in his chest. His woman was behind him. "You will step aside and allow Kathryn to pass."

Mennoc waggled his sword. "We merely want to talk to her and get to know her better."

Kathryn pushed her way in front of him. "I have no desire to talk to you. Any of you." Her gaze swept the men who now blocked their way. She lifted an eyebrow. "And in this instance, mine is the only opinion that matters."

Marc fought to hold back the grin that threatened. Damn but she was a spirited woman. Mennoc frowned and then scowled. "By law we are allowed to challenge."

"You may challenge but that does not mean you will win," Marc shot back. He wrapped his arm around Kathryn's shoulders and they continued forward. The Fairmount brothers stood their ground with the Forrester family behind them. Out of the corner of his eye he could see the Nardor brothers watching with interest.

Mennoc's sword lowered to halt their passage. Before anyone could react, another sword shot out, twisting beneath Mennoc's blade and sending it flying into the air, where it clattered as it hit the wall and fell to the floor. It was a daring move and a quick one. Marc's gaze darted to his left, expecting to see his brother. Instead it was Logan who stepped forward, the tip of his blade level with Mennoc's heart.

"The woman does not wish to speak with you." Logan's voice was low but all in the room could hear the menace in it.

"You are a stranger here," Mennoc sputtered. "You do not know our laws."

"I care not for your laws. The only thing that matters is Kathryn." He pricked the other man's skin and a thin line of blood trickled down his chest. "That is *my* law. Do you understand?"

Mennoc nodded and stepped away. Logan nodded but did not lower his blade until Marc and Tienan had ushered Kathryn back up the stairs.

She was shaking almost uncontrollably by the time they reached her room. "I can't believe them." She slammed into the room. "Who the hell do they think they are? They can't just claim me because they want me." She glared at Marc. "Your world has serious problems."

"And yours does not?" he countered back. He was furious. The actions of the men below had made her even more determined than ever to leave.

"At least I understand my world," she muttered, absently rubbing her stomach. "Sometimes…"

Marc's anger fled. "Your belly is paining again." He ushered her over to the bed. "You should rest. Mara will be up shortly with something to ease your stomach."

She started to protest and then subsided. "I'd like to be alone for a while."

Every cell in Marc's body rebelled against this but he knew she needed this time. He had plans for later but first he wanted to talk with Logan and Tienan. He cupped her face in his hands. "Promise me you'll rest."

Her expression softened and she sighed. "I promise."

"Everything will work out." He'd make certain of it.

She closed her eyes and shook her head slightly. "I don't think anything will ever be all right again." Pulling away from his grasp, she turned away from him, curling on her side on the bed.

He pulled a fur over her body, hesitating before leaning down to kiss the top of her head. "Rest. I'll be back in an hour or so." He'd need that much time to talk to Tienan and Logan and to respond to the challenges that would be put forth.

Gesturing to the other men, they all left the guest room, closing the door behind them. They were a grim trio as they went down the hallway to Marc's room where the men had passed the night.

Tienan spoke first. "What's going on? What do they mean when they said that they want to claim Kathryn?"

Marc motioned for them to sit. Tienan threw himself down onto a chair, Logan leaned against the wall and Marc propped himself up against the fireplace mantle. In simple, concise words, he explained about Javara and the history of the tapestry.

He told them how women were scarce in this world and brothers competed for a bride. Only one man could marry the woman but she would spend one night a week with each of his brothers. That way no man did without and peace was kept among all. There was one woman to no more than three men, so if there were four brothers in a family, they had the right to claim two brides. And if the husband was killed or died, the woman still had the protection of the brother, whom she could then wed if she desired.

The tapestry was a gift from a sorceress. It appeared once each generation and on the rare occasion, twice. A tapestry bride was thought to bring luck to the family and the union always bore female children, which was important to all. This third time was unprecedented in their history and no one knew what it meant. The tapestry had never taken one of them away from Javara. Marc was the first.

Tienan contemplated Marc for a few moments before speaking. "If I'm understanding your laws, it is illegal for you to claim Kathryn."

Marc's heart clenched, but he ignored the pain. "It does not matter." He would break any law, do whatever it took, to be with her.

Tienan stroked his hand over his chin. "It might all be moot anyway. Kathryn will want to return home." He paused and his green eyes bored into Marc. "If you want her to stay, you'll have a battle on your hands, both with Kathryn and with the laws of your land."

All three men were silent as they pondered everything.

"So Christina came from earth?" Logan pushed away from the wall and strolled over to the table. He went straight to the tankard of ale and poured some into three of the four cups that sat beside it. Picking up two, he handed them to the other men before retrieving his own.

"Yes. And so did Jane, wife of Zaren and Bador Bakra."

"And they are fine with this situation." Tienan held his cup in his hand, not drinking.

"Jane is very happy from what I have seen and so is Christina." Marc paused and took a sip from his cup before setting it on the mantle. "I'm the one who is not content. Although I was raised to expect and accept this, I cannot. Christina belongs to Jarek. I have not sought her out for more than a year." It was important for these men to understand that he was not attached to Christina as a lover but as a friend.

Logan shook his head. "I cannot see Kathryn being happy in such a situation."

"Nor can I," Tienan agreed.

"I want Kathryn for myself." He saw no point in holding anything back from these men. He wanted them to know where he stood.

"I kinda figured that out for myself." Logan saluted him with his glass, tipping it up and draining it before lowering it to the table with a thump. "Problem is, I want her too."

"So do I." Tienan pushed to his feet, hands on his hips. "I have wanted her for years but did not dare to make it known until recently." He glanced at Logan. "Neither of us dared. The situation would have been too dangerous for her. Our claim is just as valid, if not more-so, than yours."

Marc didn't bother to dispute their claim. He knew it was true. Both Tienan and Logan had the right to try to win Kathryn's love and affection. "It must be her choice." On that point he would not waver. Marc's insides were tied up in knots. He'd wanted to avoid this but knew it had to happen. "Kathryn is very fond of both of you. She is also attracted to you." He almost choked on the words.

"What are you suggesting?" Tienan's eyes narrowed. Marc could tell the other man was weighing and measuring his every word.

Marc pushed away from the mantle, taking the measure of the men in front of him. They were worthy adversaries. He didn't want to like them but he did. Their devotion to Kathryn was obvious and they put her safety above their own. He had a feeling that if he knew them better, they could be friends.

"That we follow the customs of Javara. The three of us will go to Kathryn tonight and pleasure her. That way, when the time comes, her choice will be made with full knowledge."

"She won't accept us all in her bed." Logan shook his head even as Marc sensed the other man's growing desire.

"Maybe not back in her world but here…" Marc let his words hang in the air.

Christina had told him much about the sexual norms on her planet. He knew what he was suggesting would be foreign in their world unless their culture had changed a great deal in the past hundred or so years. "Here it is totally acceptable and expected." His heart pounded heavily and he wanted to fight, to work off the excess anger flooding his veins. "I have seen her looking at you both. She will accept you and welcome all of us." Marc knew it had to be this way. Otherwise he'd never be sure of Kathryn if she stayed.

And if she left...

He couldn't even fathom the possibility. For the first time, he began to entertain a different idea. If she wouldn't stay, perhaps he could go with her when she left. She was not safe in her world but he could fight by her side. Tienan and Logan would teach him to use those strange weapons that he'd seen. Even if he died in that strange world, he'd be with her. Leaving behind his family and his home would be hard but losing Kathryn would be like losing himself. He would not survive.

He stepped forward. "Are you with me?"

Logan nodded. Marc turned to Tienan.

"I'm in," Tienan replied, rubbing his hand thoughtfully over his jaw. "Although I still think that you're wrong about her accepting all three of us in her bed."

Marc shook his head. "She already has, or do you not remember the dream?"

Both men appeared shocked and then Logan smiled. It was filled with male satisfaction and a hint of anticipation. "She has, hasn't she?"

* * * * *

Kathryn had waited until the door closed before rolling over onto her back and staring at the ceiling. She couldn't believe the debacle she'd just experienced. While she understood their want of a woman, the way they were going about it almost guaranteed that any sane woman was going to run in the opposite direction.

She turned onto her side and something dug in to her stomach. The journal. Sitting up, she reached into her pocket and pulled out the small leather volume. She stared at it for a long time. Somehow she knew she'd find answers in there.

Sliding off the bed, she padded over to the window seat where the light was better. The colorful panel was a thing of beauty, depicting a garden scene. She traced her fingers over the vibrant reds, blues, yellows and greens before settling on the seat.

Opening the journal, she began to read. Page after page, she scanned, the story unfolding. Seems her ancestor was a sorceress, if one believed in such things. A few days ago, Kathryn would have scoffed at the idea. A woman of science, she dealt in the facts. But she was also smart enough to know that there were many unexplained and undiscovered things in her world and beyond.

She was living proof that there was such a thing as travel across time and space and her ancestor was responsible for it. The woman talked about living in various worlds, in different times. Whether it was fact or fiction, it made for fascinating reading.

The woman, whose name was Sarainta, had apparently lived in Javara for a while. Though she had decided not to stay, she had been moved by the plight of the people and the ingenious solution they'd created for dealing with it. Using her magic, she'd created the tapestry to travel to other places and times and bring to Javara women who did not fit in their own time but who might flourish here. One per generation, maybe two. The decision belonged to the tapestry. If it could find two women, it could offer them the choice.

Kathryn curled up, resting her head against the stone wall as she thought about the science behind time travel. It boggled the mind. Turning her attention back to the book, she began reading once again.

Her eyes widened as she read about the various brides who'd been brought here over the years. Gasping, her fingers gripping the book tightly, she read about Christina and how Sarainta had enticed the other woman to buy the tapestry. She detailed the story of Jane Bakra, formerly Jane Smith, whom Kathryn had yet to meet. Her story was as amazing as Christina's. She also explained the book in the attic. Apparently, Sarainta had befriended a writer and gifted her with the stories, encouraging her to tell them. The writer had believed them to be nothing but fanciful stories of fiction but had agreed to tell the fantastic tales, enthralled by the unique tales of love and devotion.

Incredible!

Kathryn rubbed her forehead in wonder. This must have been written around the same time Christina actually arrived in Javara. That was over a hundred years in earth time but Christina had only been here for about six years. Time was fluid and it seemed that the tapestry and her ancestor had been able to move easily through time and space.

Totally enthralled, she continued to read until she stumbled across her own name. Heart pounding, she read her own story on the pages. It detailed everything, including the battle in which Marc appeared and her own journey to Javara. What it didn't have was an ending. The story abruptly stopped after it detailed her finding the journal and reading it.

Okay, now she was totally freaked out. This wasn't possible. Yet it was there in black and white. She almost tossed the book away but at the last second flipped through the remaining pages, stopping when she saw more writing.

Her eyes flew over the sheets, absorbing everything. Ohmigod! The secret of the tapestry was in the book. It was so simple if you knew the secret and accepted that there was such a thing as magic.

Kathryn swallowed as she read the final lines aloud. "This is my legacy to you but it is your choice. You are of my blood. The only living descendant of my line on Earth. Whether you go or stay, you will have the knowledge of the tapestry to help and guide you. It is a portal to other worlds if you but know its secret. Trust that the tapestry would never have brought you here if you could not find happiness in this

109

world. The tapestry has an intellect and a life all its own. You are but a guide but as you alone are of my blood, you can call it to you if necessary."

Stunned, Kathryn read the final instructions at the bottom of the page. Standing, she staggered slightly when a pain much like pins and needles poking at her went through her leg. She'd been sitting on it for a long time. The sun had passed its peak in the sky and the afternoon was waning. Kathryn knew that her time alone would soon come to an end.

Stumbling over to the fireplace, she stirred the embers, carefully adding several tiny pieces of kindling to it until she got a small flame. Slowly, she knelt and stared into the fire as it snapped and reached higher. She took a deep breath and ripped the final pages from the leather book and fed them one at a time into the flames. The fire greedily consumed them, protecting their secrets forever.

When it was done, Kathryn sat before the tiny blaze, her mind spinning with the possibilities. She could travel through time and space. She could go home or she could try her luck in a totally different world. Or she could stay here.

Her fingers tightened around the journal as Marc's face popped into her mind. All day, her thoughts had gone to him again and again. But the laws of the land would not allow her to remain with him. Tears pricked her eyes but she blinked them back. There was no time for that now.

Suddenly, she heard a commotion outside. Pushing to her feet, she went back to the window. Kathryn placed her nose against the glass, peering through the few clear pieces of glass. There was a huge crowd gathering in the courtyard below.

"They wouldn't." With her obsession with reading the journal, she'd forgotten all about the men issuing challenges earlier. She knew what that meant. A fight. Possibly to the death, with Marc right in the thick of things.

What had she missed while she'd been hiding away in her room? Because that's what she'd been doing, she realized. Hiding.

Well, the time had come to face the reality of the situation. She'd faced down worse and survived. She could do this. But, her heart screamed that she'd never had this much to lose before. Although she was attracted to Tienan and Logan, she had deeper feelings for Marc. It might seem impossible but then this entire situation was impossible. What was one more thing?

There was one heavy thud on the door and it was shoved open. Christina, her face pale, rushed into the room. "You have to come with me."

Chapter Nine

ဢ

Standing in the courtyard, Marc swung his sword, testing it, feeling the perfectly balanced blade cut through the air. It was an extension of his hand, a weapon he'd used many times before. There was a light breeze but the sun was shining. The air was sweet with the smell of freshly cut hay, overlaid with the scent of leather, sweat and horses. His long hair was tied back at his nape and he'd discarded his vest. His boots and leather pants fit comfortably and his wrists and upper arms were sheathed in strong, metal bands. A sense of rightness and calm descended upon him. This was his destiny.

"Are you certain?" His brother stood by his side, ready to support him but Marc could see the concern in Jarek's face. He loved and respected his brother, had watched his back and followed him into battle many times. Now it was Jarek's turn to watch and wait while Marc fought.

"There is no other choice. Kathryn is mine."

Jarek's piercing brown eyes narrowed as he watched the gathering crowd. A dog barked in the distance and the murmur of the crowd grew louder. The clang of metal and the swish of blades being tested filled the air as several groups of men readied themselves and their champion to fight. "What about Christina?" It was a casual question but Marc sensed the turbulence underlying his brother's words.

"Christina has always been yours." This time when he said the words there was no emptiness in his heart, for Kathryn had filled it. Marc had gone to his two nephews earlier, giving them one final hug before they were sent off with Mara. He expected to win but he wanted to say goodbye just in case. The outcome of any fight was never one hundred percent certain.

Their conversation was cut short as Tienan strode up to them, Logan by his side. Both men looked determined and Tienan appeared more than ready to fight even with the bandage wrapped around his shoulder. Looking at him, you'd never know that the man had been close to death just a day before. His powers of recovery were phenomenal. "We will fight beside you."

Marc shook his head. "That is not the way it is done. Each family will chose a champion and I will fight them. However," he continued as Tienan started to interrupt. "I would value having you watch my back in case someone gets a bit overzealous and tries to interfere."

Tienan's eyes narrowed and his lips thinned. "That is hardly fair. Kathryn was ours to protect long before you knew her."

That reminder made Marc scowl. The fact that they had a history with Kathryn left him unsettled. He could fight for her but she could still choose one of the other men. Or she might simply decide to return home. His fingers tightened around his sword hilt and he forced them to relax. Now was not the time to allow emotion to take over. That would only hinder him as he fought.

Mennoc Fairmount swaggered forward, his three brothers behind him. "Come and meet your death, Garen. We would be on our way with our new bride." The crowd roared, some of them booing Mennoc, while others cheered him. His brother Enoc laughed, his blue eyes glittering with a combination of anger and lust.

Marc strode to the center of the clearing, confident that the fight would be fair. His brother was guarding his back, along with Tienan and Logan. As well, the Bakra brothers had pledged their support. The Fairmount brothers had brought a contingent of their own men with them, as had all the visiting families but the castle guard watched them carefully. Everything was ready.

Jarek raised his hand and the crowd subsided, growing quiet. "The tapestry has blessed this land once again by bringing a potential bride." The crowd roared again.

Studying his opponent, Marc waited for his brother to dispense with the formalities so they could get on with it.

"This is a fight to see who might claim Kathryn Piedmont." Again the crowd went wild at Jarek's words. "But the choice ultimately belongs to her. The power of the tapestry will not be denied." Men muttered but they all nodded. None could deny the power of the magic.

"She will stay," Mennoc spat. "I will destroy the tapestry."

"Foolish words from one who has never felt its power." Marc raised his sword, ready to fight.

Mennoc's eyes narrowed as he circled slowly to gain a better position from which to strike. They all knew that the tapestry had taken Marc to Kathryn. That was his best claim at the moment. That and the fact that Kathryn had allowed him into her bed.

Thoughts of Kathryn, naked and writhing beneath him, filled his mind. He swore that he could almost smell her fragrant skin, tinged with her arousal. His cock stirred and he shook himself to bring his attention back to the present. Daydreams at a time like this could well lead to his death. His opponent might not be the best of men but he was a damn good fighter. Marc tracked the other man's every movement, shifting carefully and watching for an opening.

"Stop this!" Kathryn's voice rang out. Marc started to glance her way and caught the flash of metal off to his left. Ducking, he rolled. The blade whooshed by his head, a sharp reminder to pay attention to the job at hand.

He attacked, driving Mennoc back toward the edge of the crowd that encircled them. The afternoon sun was bright, so

Marc tried to keep it behind him lest it temporarily blind him. Mennoc was trying to do the same.

The air was cool but a layer of perspiration coated his chest and arms as their blades met in a clash of steel and sparks. They battled on and the crowd cheered with each well-struck blow.

Marc's sword slipped under Mennoc's guard, drawing first blood from the other man's neck. Swearing, Mennoc surged forward, renewing his attack with a ferocity that was astounding. Marc countered every move, every strike. The calmness that had enveloped him earlier remained, allowing his mind to be quick and his reflexes lightning-fast.

Kathryn. He was fighting for her and for the future he hoped they'd have together. Whether here in Javara or back in her world, Marc was determined to be at her side for whatever time the gods granted them.

A scream ripped through the air. *Kathryn!* Marc swiveled around just in time to catch a glimpse of one of the Forrester brothers trying to abduct her. The crowd surged forward and Marc lost sight of her. Mennoc let out a roar and Marc flung himself to the side, hitting the ground and rolling back to his feet.

"Go to her!" he roared. Tienan and Logan were already moving toward her. Jarek hesitated and Marc met his brother's gaze. "Go!" Jarek nodded and started to fight his way through the crowd.

He had to get to Kathryn and Mennoc Fairmount was in his way. Roaring a battle cry, Marc struck hard and fast, attacking his opponent. He drove Mennoc back, giving no ground and no quarter. He slipped under his guard, drawing blood again and again. Mennoc continued to fall back.

The crowd was out of control, many enjoying the fight, while others sought to get to Kathryn. Glancing around, Marc found himself surrounded by Mennoc and his three brothers. He'd allowed himself to be drawn into a trap. He wouldn't be surprised if the Forrester and Fairmount brothers had planned this little surprise, planning to fight amongst themselves for Kathryn once they'd killed him and spirited her away.

Marc attacked the youngest brother who was moving in on his left. Peteer was good but Marc was better. His blade bit into his opponent's shoulder and Marc swooped in, knocking the sword from Peteer's hand and grabbing it up in his left. With a blade in both hands, he swung around and headed for where he'd seen Kathryn last. He'd deal with the Fairmount Brothers after she was safe.

Sweat stung his eyes as he pushed his way through the crowd. He could hear her now, swearing and yelling as people gave way to his advance. Mennoc and his brothers would be close behind him. He didn't have much time.

One of the Forrester brothers had his forearm wrapped around Kathryn's chest, holding a blade to her throat. Jarek was currently beating back two of the Forrester's men, while Tienan and Logan engaged the other brothers.

Any doubts Marc might have had about the abilities of Kathryn's friends disappeared. The men fought like demons but with a cold, calculating skill that was brilliant to watch. They attacked, jumping high and bending their bodies at almost impossible angles to avoid counterattacks. They used their feet as well and Logan sent his opponent flying with a solid kick to the midsection.

Neither man showed any mercy. Within seconds, two of the Forrester brothers were on the ground bleeding. Marc wasn't sure if they were alive or not and didn't care. They'd touched Kathryn with intentions to kidnap and harm her.

He met Kathryn's gaze and her eyes went behind him, widening in fear. He swung around, both swords raised. Heavy blades crashed along his as both Mennoc and Enoc attacked. The entire courtyard was one bloody melee, with skirmishes all around him. A cacophony of angry voices and the sounds of blades clashing filled the air.

A far cry from the celebration of two days before.

One eye on Kathryn and the other on his opponents, he fought with everything he had. With a swift flick of his wrist, he sent Enoc's blade flying and wounded him in his side. Enoc fell to his knees in the dirt, holding his side and Marc turned his attention to Mennoc.

He sensed Jarek come alongside him. "Go to Kathryn."

Marc didn't hesitate but ducked away, knowing his brother would deal with Mennoc. The middle Forrester brother, Ormond, still held her tight in his grasp. Marc was sweating profusely now, as Logan and Tienan moved in closer, like wild animals getting ready to bring down their prey.

"Ormond!" The man jerked his head up, his fingers clutching the blade tighter. "You know you cannot hurt her." He kept his voice low and steady, not wanting to upset the delicate balance of the situation.

Anger and despair filled Ormond's eyes. "She belongs with us, not with you. Your family already has a bride, a tapestry bride."

"I know you long for a woman but this is not the way. Can you not see you are hurting her, frightening her?" Ormond glanced down at Kathryn, who appeared more angry than scared. Her nails dug into her captor's forearm and her eyes blazed with fury.

He licked his lips. "She would like it with us. Forrester Castle is a beautiful place."

"That is her choice to make, Ormond. Release her." Marc lowered his weapons and strode toward them. Dropping the sword in his left hand, he reached out to Kathryn. "Release her."

Ormond's knife eased from Kathryn's neck and it was then she struck. She jerked her elbow quickly, sending it into her captor's solar plexus. Turning in one fluid motion, she tore out of his grip and kicked him in the back of the knee. As

Ormond crumpled to the ground, Marc grabbed Kathryn, yanking her against his chest.

She was shaking uncontrollably. He didn't know if it was from fear or anger or a combination of both. Most likely the latter.

Jarek's voice filled the courtyard. "Enough." All around, the fighting stopped and men cautiously lowered their weapons. "This challenge was not met honorably. The Fairmounts and the Forresters have cheated and dishonored their family names and their homes. They are disqualified from competition and must leave. Now."

Marc heard several grunts of approval around him. Ormond and his men gathered his two wounded brothers and they hurried off toward the stables, followed by a contingent of Garen men. The Forrester brothers were being herded away by loyal Bakra men.

"What about the rest of us?" Abrah Dannon, a tall, dark-haired warrior stepped forward, his brother Heroc by his side. The Dannon brothers were good men, liked and respected by all.

Marc moved through the crowd with Kathryn tucked beneath his arm. Tienan and Logan flanked them as they moved up the stairs to stand beside Jarek. "I will meet all challengers."

Abrah nodded, satisfied by the reply.

"No." The word was little more than a whisper from Kathryn. He glanced down, noting her hands were fisted by her sides. When she raised her head, her green eyes were flashing with anger.

"No." Her voice was louder as she stepped from beneath his arm, leaving him feeling bereft. Some of her hair had come loose from her braid, creating a red halo around her face as the sun shone through it.

She glared at Abrah. "What gives you the right to challenge for me?"

"It is the law of the tapestry. It has always been thus," he countered, taking a step closer.

"The law of the tapestry," Kathryn repeated slowly, as if tasting and digesting his words.

Marc stood solidly beside her, ready to protect and support her. He wanted this done so he could take her away from all the carnage around them. They needed time alone to talk. Marc was very afraid that this incident had set the death knell to her remaining here with him.

No matter. He would go with her to her world if that's what it took and if she would have him. Resolved, he held his sword at his side, his eyes tracking all those around them. He would protect Kathryn and stay by her side until his dying breath.

Kathryn stared at the tall dark-haired man in front of her, unable to quite believe her ears. "The law," she said again, licking her dry lips.

The man nodded.

"The law certainly did not help this day, did it?" She didn't wait for a reply but swiveled so she was staring out over the courtyard. All the men watched her with lust in their eyes. Several were wounded and almost all were bloodstained.

"You cannot judge us all by the actions of a few men."

She turned back to the man who stood just beyond her. "Who are you?"

"Abrah Dannon," he replied, his voice low and even. There was a calmness that seemed to surround the man but underlying it, Kathryn felt a swell of determination.

"Well Abrah Dannon, I can do as I please." She turned aside and faced the crowd once again. It was almost eerie how quiet they were now, considering the anguished cries and acts of anger of only moments before.

She started to sway and locked her knees to keep from falling and disgracing herself. The last thing she wanted was to appear weak in front of these men. She had to appear strong and confident at all costs if what she was about to do would have a hope in hell of working.

Marc's strong arm came around her waist and she felt his powerful chest against her back. She didn't even question how she knew it was Marc. She recognized his touch, his scent, his very essence. She was glad for his support and comfort and drew strength from him.

"What you all seem to have failed to remember is that I can leave here if I choose. No matter where you take me, the tapestry will find me."

"How can you be sure?" some man shouted from the crowd.

"It has always been thus," Marc countered. "You know that, Asher."

The crowd grumbled. Kathryn squared her shoulders. "I know because I am a direct descendent of the sorceress who created the tapestry."

The crowd let out a roar of disbelief and several men surged forward. Marc tightened his hold, raising his sword in front of her. Logan, Tienan, Jarek and a host of other men stepped forward. Even the man who'd questioned her earlier, Abrah Dannon, stepped up beside Jarek to protect her. This could easily fall into another bloody melee, this one even worse than the first.

"Stop!" she yelled, raising her hands as she did so. The men immediately subsided and she could see the fear in some of their eyes. Did they think she had the powers of her ancestor the sorceress?

Heart pounding, she reached into her pocket and drew out the leather journal, holding it high in the air. "This diary came with me when the tapestry brought me. It tells of the creation of the tapestry, as well as the tales of all the tapestry brides that it has brought." She paused for dramatic effect. "It ends with me." The heat of the sun beat down upon her head. Even though the air was cool, sweat beaded on her forehead, rolling down her temple. She could feel the heavy thud of Marc's heart against her back, he was pressed there so tightly.

Several men shuffled their feet, their fingers caressing the hilts of their swords but no one stepped forward. The air was charged with expectation. Kathryn could almost feel the electricity snapping in the wind that surrounded her.

"Hear me and hear me well." Clasping the journal in both hands, she held it out to the crowd, turning slowly so all could see. "There was more in the back of the book. A gift to me from the sorceress herself. I know the secret of the tapestry." She felt Marc's jerk of surprise but he never moved from his position behind her.

"Give me that book," one man roared.

"It will do you no good," she countered. "I have torn out those pages and burned them."

"It is lost," Abrah breathed.

"No," she shook her head, glancing his way. "It is not lost. I remember it all word for word. And even if I could not, what woman would want to remain here given the display you all put on this afternoon? Men wounded, some almost mortally and for what? You cannot make me feel what is not there. The tapestry is alive and has an intellect all its own. It brings women from other places to Javara, women who have the chance at thriving and being happy here. But it brings the women to where they are supposed to be."

She let them chew on that fact for a moment. The fight seemed to go out of them and many of them lowered their swords, some even sheathing them. Marc eased his sword back to his side but she sensed he was still poised and ready to use it. "When did you find this?" he whispered in her ear.

She sensed the hurt underlying his words and she felt an overwhelming need to assure him that she wasn't keeping things from him. Although why she should feel that way, she wasn't quite sure. Still, she couldn't shake the feeling. "Just before Christina came and got me," she whispered back, under her breath.

His fingers shifted, tightening against her belly. Immediately, heat shot between her thighs and she closed her eyes, swallowing heavily. Now was not the time or the place but that didn't seem to matter. When it came to Marc, her body had a mind of its own.

The quicker this was done, the sooner she could retire to her room. She felt dusty and lightheaded. She'd hardly eaten anything these past two days. That coupled with the emotional overload and the physical strain of the afternoon, it was a wonder she was still on her feet.

Clearing her throat, she continued to address the crowd. "If a woman is brought to a particular family, then that is where she was meant to be. Taking her elsewhere will only ensure that she leaves. If there is a chance she will stay, then she needs to stay with the family she was brought to and given the chance to know those men."

She tried to think of a way to help them understand more fully the challenge these women faced. "Imagine if your sisters or daughters were ripped from all they knew and deposited in a strange world. Furthermore, they were told that they had to sleep with men they'd never met and pick a husband. Plus, this all had to happen in three days, and if they couldn't make a decision, the tapestry would do it for them."

Several of the men in front of her appeared more thoughtful. "Think if *you* were ripped from all that you know and sent to a world where everything was different."

Marc shifted behind her and she felt the rumble of his voice against her back as he began to speak. "You all know that the tapestry took me from here."

Once again the crowd rumbled and many of the men nodded.

"I did not see much of Kathryn's world but there were weapons that were unknown to me. Powerful things that

could kill a man without even having to get close to him."
Marc sucked in a large breath, letting it out slowly. "My skills
were all but useless there. If not for the element of surprise, I
would probably be dead."

She heard Jarek's cry of denial, even as she knew Marc
spoke the truth. The thought of him injured or dead was
almost too much for her to bear. She bit her lip to keep from
crying. She longed to wrap her arms around his waist and
bury her face against his chest. But now was not the time.

"Marc speaks the truth." Kathryn slowly turned her head
so she could see Tienan as he spoke. "Guns, they're called. For
some reason they didn't come with us when the tapestry
brought us here and that isn't a bad thing. In our world, there
are weapons that could blow a hole in the side of the castle in a
matter of seconds. It's a brutal place." Tienan paused. "Yet
there is much good there too." Reaching out, he stroked the
side of her face.

Kathryn stretched her hand up to touch his, their fingers
entwining. She hadn't forgotten that their world was still in
turmoil, waiting for them to return. Sighing, she forced herself
to move, knowing she had to finish this.

There were women and children in the crowd now,
drawn by the drama of what was unfolding. She saw Christina
was beside Jarek and the Bakra wives had joined their
husbands.

"I know that the laws of your land are for the protection
and happiness of all, but the tapestry is magic, it does not
recognize your laws. The tapestry is what it is and you must
accept the decisions it makes."

"And if we don't," one man countered.

"Then I can make certain that the tapestry never returns
here." Kathryn waited for the explosion, which wasn't long
coming.

Men yelled and protested but underneath it all she sensed
panic and fear. It was then that she realized that these were

mostly good men who only wanted wives and children. Families of their own.

She started to step away from Marc but his arm tightened around her. He wasn't hurting her but she was locked in his embrace. "I have to do this," she murmured. She felt his reluctance as his muscles slowly uncoiled and his forearm fell back to his side. "Thank you."

Kathryn took the five steps that led her up to the large stone landing in front of the heavy oak castle door. Stuffing the journal in her pocket, she faced the west where the sun was a blinding ball of orange in the sky. The afternoon was half gone and it would begin its descent behind the mountains in the distance within a few short hours.

She began to chant the words under her breath, having no idea if this would work. As a woman of science and reason, she felt half foolish thinking that a few spoken words could actually make the tapestry appear. As a woman who'd experienced all she had the past two days, she knew that anything was possible.

Opening her heart and her mind to the magic, she shut out the scene around her and concentrated on the words that had been written in the journal. They were a mishmash of languages—Latin, Arabic, French and some she'd never spoken before. Yet she knew how to pronounce them and their meaning. That in itself was magic. It also bespoke of the unassailable fact that her ancestor had traveled to many different places, some on Earth and some on unknown planets.

The air began to swirl around her and she could almost hear a voice on the wind. She began to chant louder and faster, the words blurring together to create more of a rhythm than individual meaning.

Lightning streaked across the pale blue sky. People screamed and yelled but no one moved as the scene unfolded around them all. The hair on her arms and on the back of her neck rose. Power filled Kathryn and she rose up on the tips of her toes as her body jerked.

She heard her name yelled in anguish. She wanted to reassure Marc that she was fine but her lips wouldn't stop chanting. It poured from her, a river of power.

Kathryn focused on the energy, channeling it the way it was meant to be. Calling on the tapestry to come. There was a blinding flash of light. She blinked to clear her vision and it was then she saw it, drifting as if held by an unseen hand in front of her.

The air all around it hummed with power. Several women screamed and Kathryn knew that the tapestry brides from this generation were frightened. Marc scrambled up the steps with Logan and Tienan hot on his heels. He grabbed her, his hold so tight she could barely breathe.

She pushed at his arm and he loosened his grip but only slightly. She could almost hear his thoughts. And if the tapestry was going to take her, he was determined to go with her.

Shocked, she froze in place. It had never even occurred to her that Marc would leave Javara and return to Earth with her. That wasn't how it was done. But hadn't they already broken every rule?

Kathryn needed to think about this.

Instead, she turned to Christina and Jane. "There is no need to fear. You have made your decision and the tapestry would never unmake it."

The tapestry drew her gaze, the design was swirling, never settling. Forests, castles and faces all came into view for a split second before disappearing. "This is the tapestry that was given to this world. It has changed the rules this time. Possibly because I am a descendant of the original sorceress, I have been given knowledge."

A woman's voice floated on the wind, spilling over the forest and the tall stone castle, swirling around the people where they stood. "This was my gift to you, yet for some of you it is not enough."

Voices protested and many men and women fell to their knees where they stood as fear overtook them. Kathryn blinked as the vision of a woman's face appeared in a large cloud. Her hair was white, yet her skin was unlined. Her eyes were sad and kindly at the same time. The cloud grew in size until her entire body was revealed, floating in the air. She appeared ageless, ethereal, her long hair flowing around her simple silver robe.

Behind her, Christina gasped. "That's the woman from the shop. The one who sold me the tapestry."

"She's the woman from the thrift store." Kathryn hadn't been introduced to the woman who spoke but she knew it had to be Jane.

Kathryn knew that this was her ancestor, the original sorceress. The resemblance to her mother was uncanny. Kathryn might not have known her mother but she'd seen pictures and the two women looked enough alike to be sisters.

"She looks like you," Marc breathed. "If your hair was white, you would be almost identical."

Now that he'd mentioned it, it made perfect sense. She looked like her mother, so she also bore an uncanny resemblance to the sorceress. The woman looked at her and smiled. "Are you enjoying my gift to you?" Her voice, though soft and melodic, reached to the far edges of the crowd.

"Ah...yes. It's been interesting."

Sarainta laughed. "You will make your choice as all tapestry brides do. Go or stay. It is your choice." Then she turned toward the crowd. "This was a gift. A thank you to your world for the time I spent here. You will accept the will of the tapestry."

As one, everyone in the crowd nodded.

"Then all is good." She returned her gaze to Kathryn. "You have one more day."

With that there was another blinding flash. Kathryn barely managed to bring her arm up to shield her eyes. Hands grabbed her, holding on tightly. When she could finally see again, both the woman and the tapestry were gone.

Marc, Tienan and Logan were holding various parts of her body. "Ah, you can let go now." Fingers and hands slowly unpeeled from her arms but Marc kept his forearm wrapped around her.

"This is done." Jarek's voice rang out authoritatively over the crowd. "You will accept the will of the tapestry and Kathryn's decision."

One by one the men and women passed her on their way back into the castle. They all nodded, most of their gazes darting away. Great. Now she felt like a freak in this world too. No matter what, she seemed destined to be different.

Abrah paused before her. Bending down, he brushed her cheek with his lips. "I will accept your decision. But, if you get tired of this group…" His eyes twinkled as he made his offer.

Kathryn rather liked the man and his brother, who stood by his side but not enough to leave Marc. "Thanks."

Marc growled behind her but she ignored him for the moment. She had a feeling he was going to have a lot to say later.

The last to stop and stand before her was Jarek, with Christina by his side. He stared down at her from his great height. "Our home is your home." Cupping her chin in his large hand, he stroked the line of her jaw. "You have brought much excitement here."

Kathryn felt her cheeks flush. Excitement, her ass. More like chaos and bloodshed.

"You make Marc happy and that means everything to me. Please consider staying. Do not let what happened here today taint your decision. Take tonight to…think about things."

She knew what he really meant was, take tonight to have hot monkey sex with Marc. Her nipples tightened and her sex clenched as if to let her know how much they approved of that idea.

"Tomorrow, tour the castle. Talk to the people here. Get to know us all before you decide."

"I will," she promised Jarek.

"That is all I can ask." He dropped his hand back by his side.

Christina stepped up and threw her arms around Kathryn. Shocked, she patted the other woman's back with awkward movements. She wasn't used to public displays of affection. "I hope you stay," Christina whispered in her ear. "I could use another woman around here, one who understands what I'm going through. Jane and I are friends but I don't get to see her as often as I'd like."

"I will make your apologies to our guests." With that, Jarek draped his arm over his wife's shoulders and they walked into the castle, leaving the four of them alone on the landing.

"What did Jarek mean?" She turned to face Marc and the undisguised lust and longing in his eyes had her body softening and her limbs shaking. A quick glance down assured her that he was fully aroused. Her mouth went dry at the thought of making love with him once again.

"He meant, sweet Kathryn, that it is time for us to retire to my room." Bending down, he licked her bottom lip before nipping it with his teeth. She gasped, blood surging through her body. Her core was moist and hot and pulsing to a primal rhythm.

"Umm…" She glanced at Tienan and Logan and wasn't shocked by the carnal gleam in their eyes. Her gaze fell and, sure enough, they were both fully aroused. "What do you mean, it's time for *us* to retire to your room?"

Marc sheathed his sword and swept her into his arms. "Just what I said. It's time for us to pleasure you. To lick every inch of your delectably soft skin, to touch every satiny curve and hollow and to pleasure you until you scream your release. Then we'll fuck you until you come again and again and again." His lips came down hard against hers, claiming her, marking her. She knew she'd never forget the taste of his mouth or the feel of his lips for as long as she lived.

When he pulled back, they were both panting for breath. He raised an eyebrow as he turned to the other two men. "You coming?"

Chapter Ten

ဢ

Although the fight was over, Marc's body was still poised and ready to react. Adrenaline pumped through his veins and he needed an outlet for all the emotions raging within him. Fear, anger, lust and love all vied for dominance.

He'd stood beside Kathryn and watched but he could still hardly credit what he'd seen. The tapestry, the sorceress, the magic and power in the air—it was the stuff of legends. Yet, he didn't care about any of it. All that mattered was the woman in his arms. He still had a night and a day to convince her to stay with him.

But he also had to give her the choice and not merely the choice between leaving and staying. She'd arrived with Tienan and Logan and it was obvious she had feelings for them. That had to be addressed if any of them were ever going to be satisfied with the outcome. Marc didn't want to be second best this time. If Kathryn chose him, he wanted it to be because she wanted him and maybe even loved him. Nothing else would do.

No matter what happened, he would stay by her side because he loved her. There was no denying his feelings. He would kill any man who threatened her. He would even face down a sorceress to keep her by his side. But he would not deny her right to choose. Still, even if she picked one of the other men or decided to return to her own time, he wanted to be part of her life. Unlike Christina, whom he knew he could live without, he now understood that there was no other woman for him but Kathryn.

"Marc?" He could hear the question in her voice as he carried her though the door of the castle and up the staircase.

The stone was solid beneath him but he felt as if he were on uneven ground. The next few hours would decide his fate.

"All will be well," he promised. "Trust me." Logan and Tienan were close behind him, listening to every word. And why not? Their fate was to be decided as well.

"I do," she whispered, resting her head against his shoulder. His cock jerked, pressing hard against his leather pants, a physical reminder of precisely how much he needed the woman in his arms.

He carried her down the hallway and into his room. If he only had this night with her, then he wanted her in his bed, spread across his sheets. His arms tightened possessively around her for a fraction of a second before he made himself relax as he crossed the threshold.

Logan went straight to the fireplace and lit the kindling. The flames crackled as they caught the wood. Tienan closed the door and went around the room, lighting all the candles. The light flickered against the walls. It wasn't dark yet but the room was dim. The candles and firelight would allow them to see Kathryn more clearly as they made love to her.

As much as he wanted to continue holding her, Marc slowly released her legs until she was standing. When he was certain she was steady, he backed away to stand beside the other two men.

"You know the laws of this land?"

"I do." She crossed her arms across her chest. She appeared tired and fragile and just looking at her hurt his heart. But this had to be done.

"You came with two men and they have a prior claim to you."

"But they don't want me. Not like that." Her eyes widened as her gaze went to her friends. Marc could tell that she didn't really believe the words she was speaking.

"Yes, we do." Tienan spoke up, his voice thick with need. "We've always wanted you, Kathryn."

She swallowed and the delicate column of her neck rippled. He wanted to kiss the vein that pulsed there. To distract himself, he unbuckled his sword belt and laid it carefully aside.

"You're an incredibly brave and beautiful woman." Logan never took his eyes from her as he stripped off his sword and placed it on the table.

"I don't understand." Kathryn took a step back, bringing her one step closer to the large bed behind her.

"It is simple." Marc released the armbands encircling his upper arms and tossed them aside. "We all want you but only one of us can be your husband. If you will allow us, we will pleasure you, so you will be able to chose which one of us you want."

"This is crazy." Her words were little more than a breathy sigh but Marc could see the excitement and growing desire in her eyes. She parted her lips, licking them. The sight of her pink tongue darting out of her mouth made his balls draw up tight against his body.

"This is perfectly natural and accepted here. You are not in your world, Kathryn. You are in mine." He felt that the only resistance to the idea was because it was not acceptable on her planet. He'd learned much from Christina about Earth and, though they were from different times, the basic accepted sexual practices did not seem to differ greatly.

"Let us touch you." Logan slid his vest off and let it fall to the floor.

Tienan moved fluidly to her other side, his white bandage stark against his swarthy skin. "I want to taste your lips, your mouth and your moist pussy."

Kathryn's mouth fell open and her breathing quickened. Her chest rose and fell with each breath, accentuating the sway of her breasts and the fact that her nipples were hard buds, outlined by the fabric of her tunic.

"Let us pleasure you." Marc stepped in front of her, so close they were almost touching. Her breasts grazed his chest with each breath she took. He stripped off his vest and tossed it aside. "Let me have you," he murmured as he leaned toward her, nuzzling her jawline.

He placed tender kisses along the curve of her neck before twirling his tongue along the delicate shell of her ear. "Let me fuck you." He was desperate now, his body throbbing, his soul crying for release that only she could give him. He kept his arms straight by his sides and his hands fisted to keep from grabbing her, tossing her on the bed, stripping her and driving his cock into her waiting heat. He wanted to pound into her body until they both shattered and yelled their release.

"Kathryn." He breathed her name and held still as he awaited her decision.

Kathryn could barely breathe, let alone think. Her mind was still reeling from everything that had just happened. Magic did exist and so did the sorceress—an ageless, powerful entity that had given her the gift of freedom and choice. But with choice came responsibility and Kathryn knew that, whatever decision she made, there would be consequences she'd have to live with for the rest of her life.

Even as she'd denied it, she'd known that all three men wanted her. She'd known that Tienan and Logan had both wanted her for a while now but she'd avoided the issue because it just wasn't possible. At least not in her world. But here…here everything was different.

When Marc breathed her name, she could hear the longing and the need in his voice and it matched the emptiness, the yearning that existed within her. Every nerve ending in her body was alive, thrumming with anticipation. She'd already made her decision. All she had to do was open her mouth and say the words.

She could sense the masculine impatience in the air and knew that most of it was coming from Logan. The man practically vibrated with emotional energy. Tienan was quieter as he awaited her decision but she could almost hear his mind working, calculating his odds of success. But Marc…Marc was stoic, ready to accept whatever choice she made without question.

It really was her decision. And that made all the difference.

"Yes." Her voice seemed unnaturally loud in the quiet of the room. "Yes," she said again, this time more softly, as she looked at the three very different men standing in front of her. She needed to make sense of her chaotic thoughts and feelings, had to know once and for all how Logan and Tienan fit into her life. Was it possible to love three men at once? She didn't think so, at least not with the same degree of emotion.

Tonight was about pleasure—hers and theirs. After all the death and destruction, she wanted to feel alive. It was also about giving, about opening herself emotionally to test the depth of her feelings for each man. They were all willing to give of themselves freely. She could do no less.

Kathryn knew this could end badly. She swallowed back the lump in her throat that threatened to choke her. She couldn't bear the thought of losing Logan's and Tienan's friendship. It was all that had gotten her through many long, lonely years. Then there was Marc. What she felt for him was so new but went so deep. She owed it to herself and to him to explore their burgeoning relationship.

The corners of Marc's mouth turned up in a smile so breathtakingly beautiful it brought tears to her eyes. The way he looked at her made her heart race. He made her feel special and sexy, as if she were the only woman in the world who could satisfy him. And maybe she was. The tapestry had a magic all its own that couldn't be denied.

She blinked to clear her vision and glanced at Tienan and Logan. They were both staring at her as if they were starving and she was lunch. A fresh gush of moisture pooled between her thighs and she shifted from one foot to the other, not quite knowing what to do next. This wasn't a situation she'd been in before. A snort of nervous laughter escaped her. Now that was an understatement.

Marc reached behind her and pulled the tail of her braid over her shoulder. He pulled the leather cord from the end and began to unwind her hair. Slowly, he combed his fingers through the long red tresses, watching as the bottoms of the strands curled slightly around his hand.

"Beautiful." The tips of his fingers massaged her scalp before easing through the mass of her hair one final time. "Like fire. I've dreamed of it spread across my pillow while my cock is buried inside your heat."

Her pussy clenched and released at his provocative words. She closed her eyes and tried to breathe but there didn't seem to be enough air left in the room. She could picture the scene perfectly. Could see his large body over hers as his hips flexed and he pumped his cock into her over and over again.

She jerked, her eyes popping open when cool air hit her stomach. Marc had her tunic halfway up her body. "Lift your arms."

She swallowed hard. Her heart pounded so loudly in her ears that she could barely hear him. Her arms inched upward as if totally independent of her will. It wasn't a conscious decision but an automatic one.

He pulled the garment over her head and let it fall from his fingers. Her bra was next. Marc reached behind her and unhooked the flimsy covering, tossing it aside. She was naked from the waist up with only her hair to cover her chest. She glanced down at her chest only to find her hardened nipples peeking out from between several thick locks.

Tienan and Logan stepped up beside Marc, one on either side. Now she had all three men looking at her breasts. She curled her toes in her shoes. Her nerve endings quivered, her sheath dampened and the slick folds thickened as blood pooled between her thighs, preparing her for what was to come.

It was Tienan who reached out first, the tip of his forefinger tracing the edges of her nipple before stroking over the nub. Her breath caught in her throat and she began to shake. The adrenaline from the fight and all that had happened crashed down on her at once. Her legs began to quiver and it climbed over her torso and down her arms until she couldn't stop.

Logan's arm went around her shoulders and she leaned into him, needing his support and comfort. Marc wasted no time in unlacing her pants and tugging both them and her underwear over her thighs and down her legs. "Lift."

She picked up her left foot and then her right as Marc tugged off her pants, underwear and shoes, leaving her naked in front of them. She shuddered violently and Logan lifted her against him as Tienan pulled back the furs on the bed.

"I don't know what's wrong with me." Even her teeth were chattering. Logan placed her carefully in the center of the gigantic bed.

"Fear, adrenaline, sexual need—it's all churning together inside you." Marc had stripped off what was left of his clothing, unbound his hair and now joined her. The mattress dipped slightly as he pulled her into his arms, running his hands over her back and shoulders and down her arms. His heat was a strong lure and she snuggled against him, burying her nose in the light dusting of hair on his chest. Even sweaty from fighting, he smelled good. He had an earthy smell of male sweat, the crisp air, leather and musk. His cock was almost hot against her belly and she could feel the pulse of it like a heartbeat. The shivers subsided and a different kind of energy filled her, leaving her restless and aching.

The covers swished and she knew that Tienan and Logan had joined them. A hand stroked down her spine and she arched like a cat. Male laughter, soft and satisfied, filled the air as the hand dipped lower to stroke her bottom. Clever fingers slid into the crease, making her jump as the tip of one finger circled the tight puckered entrance of her behind.

She glanced over her shoulder. Tienan grinned at her as he pushed his hand deeper. His fingers brushed over her slick folds and she sucked in a breath, her nails digging into Marc's biceps.

Logan settled higher on the bed, watching. He leaned down and brushed a kiss on her nape before sliding his hand over her shoulder and around front to cup her breast. "Let us pleasure you, Kathryn."

She'd never heard him say her name like that before, filled with such yearning. She turned back to Marc, needing to gauge his reaction. Uncertainty filled her. What the heck was she doing?

As if sensing her unease, Marc stroked his fingers down the side of her face. "Let us give you what you need."

She swallowed heavily and nodded. She'd made her decision, but more than that, she knew that if she didn't do this, she'd have regrets for the rest of her life. From the first moment she'd read Christina's story, she'd been filled with curiosity and a rising desire to know what it felt like to be loved by more than one man at once. This was her opportunity. This was her time. Who knew what tomorrow would bring? Tonight nothing else mattered but the four of them in this room together.

Capturing Marc's face in her hands, she tugged him down until their mouths were touching. Parting her lips, she offered him everything she was, giving him permission to do whatever he would. She trusted him. She trusted all three of them. In her own way, she loved all three, but deep down, she was afraid that Marc owned her heart, body and soul.

Shoving aside those thoughts, she concentrated on their kiss. Tonight was all about pleasure. Tomorrow she would deal with the consequences.

Their tongues touched and twined together as Marc angled her face and deepened the contact. He tasted masculine and wild and she couldn't get enough of him. When he finally released her, she licked her lips, wanting to capture his unique flavor, wanting to remember it always, no matter what happened.

He eased her onto her back and started to shift aside. She grabbed his hand. "Don't leave me." She wanted Marc beside her, needed the connection with him. He gave her the courage to reach out to the other two men who waited.

"I won't," he assured her, bringing her fingers to his lips. The moist warmth of his mouth caressed each knuckle in turn before he placed a kiss in the center of her palm.

Fingers gently brushed a strand of hair from her forehead. "Kathryn?" Logan waited patiently as she turned to face him. He offered her a smile tinged with sadness even as he leaned toward her. Her breath hitched as he covered her mouth with his.

Heat exploded as he leisurely explored every crevice of her mouth. He stroked her teeth, her tongue and the top of her mouth, taking the time to make certain that not one tiny place was forgotten. His mouth was hot, his lips soft. Groaning, she surrendered to the embrace.

She felt Marc's hand on her hip as her legs shifted restlessly. His hand slid down the back of her thigh. Lifting her leg, he draped it over Logan's hip. Logan moaned and captured her leg, pulling it even higher.

Her breasts pressed against Logan's broad chest and she arched her back, rubbing her nipples against the hard muscles. She gasped and Logan captured the sound in his mouth as he continued to consume her with his kiss.

"Enough," Tienan growled.

Logan reluctantly released her, nuzzling his nose against hers before he pressed her onto her back. With Logan and Marc on either side of her, Tienan sat at her feet. He pushed her legs apart and made a space for himself between them. Bracing his hands by her shoulders, he crouched over her like some large beast ready to devour her.

And that's exactly what he did.

While Marc's kiss was passionate and loving and Logan's was hot and thorough, Tienan consumed her. There was no soft, tentative exploration. Tienan captured her mouth and boldly laid claim to her. When he pulled away, he was panting heavily, a strand of his dark hair plastered against his forehead. Possessiveness was etched on every inch of his face. He sat back slowly, glancing at the other two men as he did so.

A low rumble came from Marc's chest as he lowered his head and captured the tip of her breast between his lips and sucked. His large hand cupped her, holding her in place as his tongue lapped at the puckered nub.

Kathryn pressed her head back against the pillows, her hips arching upward as Logan captured her other breast in his large hand and began to lick the plump flesh. His tongue was slightly rough and very arousing.

Her entire body was flooded with sensation. Then she felt hot breath against her core. She cried out as Tienan licked at her sensitive folds. "I knew your pussy would taste sweet," he muttered as he licked and sucked his way up one side and down the other, all the while avoiding her clitoris.

She bucked her hips toward him, needing that contact. Her breasts and pussy were alive with sensation and she knew she was close to coming. Her body screamed for release as the three men continued to practice their sensual torture on her. "Please," she panted, planting her feet on the bed and pushing her core toward Tienan's waiting mouth. "Please," she managed to gasp again.

She was so close it was almost unbearable.

Tienan captured her clit and sucked at the same moment that the other two men did the same at her breasts. Kathryn screamed. Like a jolt of electricity had been shot into her body, she jerked and shook.

Reaching out, she grabbed Marc's hand, needing something to ground her. He released her breast and she rolled into his arms. Gradually the aftershocks diminished and she became aware of being surrounded by masculine heat. A hard cock pressed against her belly, another against her back. She could feel the dampness against her as both erections leaked from the tip, proclaiming their readiness to take her.

A spark began to heat her core once again and her pussy clenched, reminding her that she hadn't been filled, hadn't been taken by any of them yet.

"How do you feel?" Marc eased her away from him and she smiled.

"I feel wonderful."

Marc smiled at her, making the corners of his eyes crinkle slightly. "Good. Because we've only just begun."

Tienan parted her thighs and shifted closer. Kathryn panicked and pulled her knees upward. He froze and slowly released her. She shook her head. "I'm sorry."

"Don't ever be sorry." He placed a kiss on her hip. "If you're not ready or don't want this, then that is your decision."

She pushed away from the mattress and came up on her knees. "I'm not sure what I want." She shoved her fingers through her hair, pushing it out of her eyes. "I want all of you but I'm not sure that I can actually go through with it."

Marc wrapped his arms around her from behind, cupping her breasts in his hands. "All we want is your pleasure."

"But that's not fair to all of you. I feel like a tease." She was frustrated and angry with herself. She wanted to do this, yet when Tienan had made to enter her, she felt as if she were cheating on Marc.

"You are not a tease." Logan slid up beside her. Like the other two men, his cock was fully erect and ready. "I'll take whatever you can give me and count myself lucky."

Kathryn had often wondered how Christina could take two men to her bed and then pick one. Now she understood. She had deep feelings for all three men. If she'd never met Marc, she might very well have had a relationship with either Tienan or Logan, or both. But she had met Marc and everything had changed.

"It is all right for them to pleasure you, Kathryn," Marc whispered in her ear, his hot breath almost making her moan.

"I don't want to hurt any of you." There, her greatest fear was out in the open. She didn't want Tienan or Logan to feel as Marc had with Christina. Second best. Left out. And there really was no way around it. She wasn't emotionally capable of loving all three men in the same way.

She hadn't realized she'd said the last aloud until Tienan captured her chin between his thumb and forefinger and raised her gaze to his. "Then love us all differently."

Surrounded by such love and acceptance, her heart swelled. She wanted to give to all of them, to please them, to share her body with them.

She looked at Marc and he nodded. Logan did the same.

Taking a deep breath, Kathryn scooted forward, rising up on her knees as she positioned herself in front of Tienan. "Take me."

Chapter Eleven

ഇ

Marc watched as Tienan's hands wrapped around Kathryn's hips, lifting her and positioning the head of his cock against her opening. Tienan's hard length slid into her supple body. Marc could practically feel it around his own erection. He knew what the other man was feeling, knew how Kathryn's slick sheath would tighten and caress his cock.

He shifted as his shaft jerked in anticipation. A part of him wanted to rip Kathryn from Tienan's grasp and ram his cock into her hot core. Another part of him was aroused by the sheer erotic picture she made as Tienan raised and lowered her over his cock. The heavy sac between Marc's thighs tightened, a reminder of how much he wanted to be the one fucking her. He gripped the base of his cock in his hand and squeezed tightly.

Kathryn's hair flowed like a curtain of fire down her back. Reaching out, he wrapped a strand around his hand, needing to touch her even as she rode another man to completion. A log in the fireplace snapped and light flared briefly before settling back to a slow, steady burn. That's what he felt like—a slow, steady burn that could flare at any moment.

He wanted to warm himself against Kathryn's fire, to absorb her heat into his body and share his with her. Her breathy moans and gasps mingled with the masculine sounds that Tienan made.

He wasn't the only one enthralled. Logan was slowly pumping his hand up and down his cock, his eyes never leaving the couple in the throes of passion.

Marc shifted closer, slipping his hands around Kathryn and cupping her breasts. She cried out as he lightly teased her nipples with his thumbs and forefingers. "Yes," she moaned as Tienan worked her harder and faster.

Her back bowed as her climax hit her. Her slender neck arched back. With her eyes closed and her moist lips parted on a cry of ecstasy, she was the picture of erotic beauty. He released her and simply watched. Marc knew that he'd never forget the way she looked at this moment. It was etched in his mind forever.

Tienan yelled his release, pumping a few more times before gathering Kathryn into his arms and hugging her tightly. A few moments later, he lifted her from him and laid her back on the mattress. Her legs splayed apart and Marc could see cum glistening on her thighs and pussy. Her eyes were still closed, her chest rising and falling rapidly as she sucked in one breath after another.

Tienan fell back against one of the thick bedposts and rested there, head bowed, lungs pumping.

Logan wasted no time and positioned himself between Kathryn's spread legs. Hooking his arms under her thighs, he lifted them toward him. Her eyes popped open and she moaned as Logan easily slid his cock into her.

Marc closed his eyes and concentrated on gaining control. He was close to coming but didn't want to spill on the sheets. It was worse with his eyes shut. The sound of the furs and sheets swishing and crinkling with each thrust, the harsh breathing and the soft gasps and the cries of pleasure all combined to create an erotic song that just about drove him mad.

And the smells. Damn, the smell of sex—a deep, heavy musk—permeated the air around him. The scents of leather and sweat mingled with a lighter, flowery fragrance that beckoned and enticed.

Opening his eyes, he watched the couple beside him. Logan had planted his hands flat on the bed. The position opened Kathryn wide and allowed Logan all the control as he

thrust into her, slowly at first, then faster, then slow once
again. He varied the depth and speed of his thrusts, pushing
Kathryn's need higher and higher.

Her eyes were open but they appeared almost blind as
her gaze seemed fixed on the passion building inside her. A
low keening sound broke from her throat as Logan pumped
his hips faster and harder, driving deep with each trust.
Kathryn wrapped her hands around Logan's arms, her
fingernails pressing deep into his flesh.

Marc knew they were both close to coming.

Logan roared, hammering his hips against Kathryn. She
screamed, tears seeping from the corners of her eyes. Marc
wanted to comfort her but knew this was Logan's time. Rolling
from the bed, he hurried to the bathing room, all the while
trying to ignore the heavy ache in his balls and the throbbing
of his cock. One wrong move and he knew he'd explode.

But Kathryn needed tending after what she'd been
through. Her body wasn't used to such an erotic workout.
Thankfully, there was some fairly warm water in a basin and
he dipped a soft cloth into it, wringing most of the water from
it as a low feminine moan drifted into the room.

Every muscle in his body jerked and tightened,
demanding he do something, demanding he claim her.
Grabbing a soft towel as well, he carried both items back into
the bedroom.

Kathryn was sprawled across his bed, the only movement
the rise and fall of her chest. Logan was flat on his back beside
her, his forearm flung over his face. Tienan continued to watch
from his post as the end of the bed, absently rubbing his
bandaged shoulder.

The fire was starting to burn low but with the candles lit
there was more than enough light for him to see her. Her
slender limbs glistened with perspiration and a bead of sweat
rolled down her forehead.

Starting between her thighs, he gently washed her swollen flesh. Her eyes flashed open at the first touch of the cloth. She watched as he washed her sex and thighs. Folding the cloth, he used a clean side to wipe her arms and legs. He should have brought a basin of water with him instead of only a cloth but he wasn't about to leave her to go get it.

The towel was clean, so he used that to wipe her face and neck. She sniffed and that was when he realized that she was crying. It wasn't beads of sweat rolling down her temples but tears.

Tossing the towel and cloth to the floor, he gathered her in his arms and leaned against the massive headboard. Kathryn curled into him, wrapping her arms around his waist. He was struck by just how delicate and fragile she felt. For all her courage, she was a woman, and as such, she was to be cherished and protected at all costs.

"Rest, little one," he murmured, wiping away a tear with the pad of his thumb.

"I'm not crying," she insisted.

"I know," he assured her, biting back a smile. His woman didn't like to appear weak at all. He could have told her that all the tears in the world wouldn't diminish her courage in his eyes.

She sniffed and wiped her face with the back of her hand before tilting her head to look at him. "What about you?"

Her words were slurred and he frowned as he noticed the dark circles under her eyes. "Don't worry about me." He brushed her temple with his hand, admiring the reddish glint of her fiery locks. "I'm fine." Which was only partially true. His cock was a throbbing ache the likes of which he'd never felt before. But he would take care of that as soon as Kathryn fell asleep.

"No." She pushed away from his chest. "I want you."

"Kathryn," he began but she cut him off.

"No." She said again as she straddled his lap, bringing her hot pussy in contact with his straining cock. The heat burned him to his very core. He needed her but not at the expense of her health and wellbeing.

"You need to rest first."

She arched against him, stroking his entire length with her sex. Breathing was almost impossible as heat raged through his body. His cock burned for her. Her breasts pressed against his chest, the tight nubs caressing him. He clenched his jaw, grasping for control. Sweat rolled down his back. His balls tightened.

"Take me," her lips whispered against his. "I need to feel you inside me."

He saw the sincerity in her eyes and knew that she was telling him the truth. She needed him.

His control snapped.

Exhaustion swamped Kathryn. All she wanted to do was sleep. But she couldn't. Not yet. She'd reached sexual fulfillment with Tienan and Logan. Both experiences were incredible but there was still an emptiness inside her.

She loved Tienan and Logan but she wasn't in love with them. She'd never known the difference until now. She loved Marc and she was in love with him. She couldn't separate the emotions filling her with the sexual release she had found with Marc.

Their relationship was impossible. He needed to stay in his world and she needed to return to her own to try to right the wrongs her father and General Caruthers had done. Their paths were divergent, only crossing in this short moment of time.

She knew all that. Had tried to protect her heart. But it was no use.

She loved Marc with ever fiber of her being.

She was a woman of science, yet sense and logic had no place here. Marc was the love of her life, the man who was meant to be hers. She needed to make love with him, to have him fill her body as they both found completion. She needed the emotional connection between them to soothe her battered soul.

And she needed it now.

Rubbing her body against his, she teased and tempted him. "Take me," her lips whispered against his. "I need to feel you inside me."

She knew he wanted her, could feel his erection throbbing against her pussy. The fact that he wanted to take care of her, was putting her wellbeing above his own needs, only made her love him more. She'd never known she could feel this way about a man. She wanted to give him what he needed. To comfort him as he did her.

His eyes narrowed, their golden-brown hue deepening. She knew the moment his control snapped. Like a tiger unleashed, he surged forward with a growl, flipping her onto her stomach. "On your hands and knees."

She felt his urge to claim her in front of the other two men who watched from the end of the bed. Kathryn settled on her hands and knees, parting her legs. Pushing her bottom toward him, she offered herself to him.

His hands were heavy on her hips but he was careful as he inserted the head of his cock into her opening. The muscles were swollen, her flesh sore, but she didn't care. She wanted him.

One slow inch at a time, he pushed his way into her. Her pussy clenched and relaxed, accepting him. Making room for him.

She sighed when he was finally buried to the hilt. When he pulled back and pushed slowly forward, she moaned. His heavy sac brushed her clit with each thrust and the light caress was driving her wild.

Leaning forward, he captured her breasts in his hands and began to pump his hips. They'd done this only last night but it felt different. As emotional as it had been before, this time was even more intense and raw. Need, tinged with an air of desperation, as if they were both aware that time grew short.

Kathryn met him stroke for stroke. Over and over he drove into her. Her sensitive inner muscles protested slightly, even as they squeezed him tightly. Squeezing her eyes closed, she shut out everything else, all her focus centered on the heavy pumping of Marc's cock between her thighs.

The heat building inside her suddenly reached a flashpoint. Crying out his name, she came. Marc thrust into her several more times and then he yelled. She felt his cock jerking inside her and the hot flood of his seed as it filled her.

She didn't want it to end but eventually the aftershocks subsided and Marc withdrew. Immediately, she felt cold and bereft and she shivered.

Marc gathered her close to his chest, neither of them speaking. Logan stretched out on her other side, pulling the heavy furs over them. Tienan was still leaning against one of the bedposts, his eyes closed.

Kathryn felt as if she should say something but words eluded her. Exhaustion hit with a finality that was inescapable. She felt herself drifting off to sleep, safe, at least for tonight, in the arms of her lover.

All through the night, Marc held Kathryn in his arms. He sensed the restlessness of the two men who shared the bed with them but he would not relinquish his hold on her. They might want and love Kathryn but she was the very breath in his body, his miracle, and he wasn't about to lose her.

The night waned and morning dawned. Marc usually loved this time of day when most of the world was still sleeping but not today. He didn't want the night to end. When the sun rose, that meant it was Kathryn's last day. The tapestry would come sometime tonight.

He snuggled her closer and she shifted, her hand drifting down his stomach and settling almost on top of his erection. He groaned as the tips of her fingers grazed his hard length. It was torture. It was heaven. He held still, not wanting to wake her. Kathryn needed to rest and eat today. She'd been through so much in the past few days. She constantly amazed him with her strength and resilience.

Her fingers twitched again, this time closing around his shaft. Her breathing changed. Quickened. The little imp was awake.

With a growl, he rolled until she was on her back, staring up at him with a soft smile. "Good morning." Her voice was slightly raspy and it skittered over his flesh like a physical caress.

He peppered her forehead, her cheeks and her nose with kisses. "Good morning."

Her hand stroked the length of his cock. "You're up early."

He snorted at her joke, pushing his hips forward, encouraging her to keep touching him. "I am."

"Seems as if we're both up early." She batted her eyelashes at him and he was charmed by her playful mood. "Whatever shall we do?"

He paused, pretending to think about it. "We could have breakfast or perhaps we could go for a walk." Her lips pursed and she shook her head. "No?" He nuzzled her neck, nibbling on her delectable skin. "Do you have any ideas?"

"Hmmm," she purred. "I've got all kinds of ideas." She pushed at his chest, so he flipped over onto his back, pulling her on top of him.

The morning light was beginning to spill through the window, casting a warm glow on her satiny skin. Her hair fell over her back and shoulders, surrounding her in a fiery halo. Her plump breasts swayed as she moved over him, the tips puckered like ripe berries, waiting to be tasted. Capturing the mounds in his hands, he thumbed her nipples, loving the soft velvety skin that surrounded the hard nub.

Kathryn placed her hands on his chest and that simple touch went straight to his groin. He loved the feel of her fingers as she stroked over the bands of muscle on his torso. Her fingers combed through the wiry hair on his chest and played over his flat nipples. He groaned and she laughed, delighted with the response.

She straddled his hips and he could feel the moist heat of her pussy against him. "Kathryn," he growled as she started to slide down his body.

"No." She shook her head, making her hair shimmer. "You've had your turn. I want to explore. To touch."

Marc knew that both Tienan and Logan were awake and watching. Had been from the moment Kathryn had stirred. "You can do whatever you want but I'm not the only one who wants you to touch them."

She seemed startled, her gaze shooting around her almost as if she'd forgotten they were here. That pleased Marc. He wanted to be the only man she thought about. But there was still one day left and until Kathryn chose, they were still in the running for her love and attention.

Kathryn felt different this morning—powerful, invigorated and alive. Last night, she'd needed the connection with the other men, needed the physical release. And they'd all given freely to her. This morning it was her turn to give to them.

This time in Javara was coming to an end. The tapestry would come today and she would go home. She was under no misconceptions about her future. She had to go back.

Didn't she?

Of course she did. She shook off the sly voice that whispered that maybe she didn't have to go back. That none of them did. They could stay here.

Yeah, look how good that turned out yesterday. Men fighting over her as if she were some prize to be awarded to the victor. Bloodshed and injury. No, she had to go back.

Her heart clenched at the thought of leaving Marc. She rubbed her chest, blinking back tears. Emotions threatened to overflow but she shoved them back. She had been incredibly emotional the past few days and she wasn't quite sure why.

Well, that wasn't entirely true. As a scientist, she could catalogue the reason why her emotions were so close to the surface. It was perfectly normal, considering all she'd been through. But it wasn't like her. She'd learned to suppress her emotions. Anything less had been unacceptable to her father. Still, the thought of losing Marc was a physical pain. If she didn't know it was physically impossible, she'd say that her heart was in danger of breaking.

"Kathryn?" She could hear the concern in Marc's voice. Sense the other men waiting to see what she would say or do.

She wouldn't think of what was to come. Not now. Now she wanted to give to the three men who'd given so freely of themselves last night.

She leaned forward until her lips were touching Marc's. Her sex pressed solidly against his erection and her breasts rubbed against his firm, muscled chest. She loved how hard he was, how strong. Yet, he was always so gentle with her. The contrast made her head spin.

"I'll be back," she whispered before going up on her knees and turning toward Logan, who was waiting patiently beside them.

His blue eyes seemed darker than usual and his short hair stood up in spikes. For once, she sensed no impatience from him but instead an all-encompassing sadness. Like her, she sensed he knew that this was a time out of time. Today would change everything for all of them. But for now, they were here.

"Good morning." She leaned into him, capturing his lips for a kiss. She sensed his surprise and pleasure and it made her smile.

His lips turned up at the corners as the simple kiss ended. "You look well rested, Kathryn."

"I feel well rested, thanks to all of you." Letting her hand stroke down his chest, she felt the muscles jump beneath her palm. "But I'm not sleepy any longer."

He rumbled like a big cat as she petted her way toward his cock, which was fully erect and straining upward, reaching for her touch. "That's good."

She didn't know if he meant it was good she wasn't sleepy any longer or what she was doing to him felt good. She suspected the latter.

Her fingers closed around his erection and squeezed. Liquid seeped from the tip and suddenly she wanted to taste him. Lowering her head, she lapped at the head of his cock. He groaned her name as his fingers dug into her scalp, holding her tightly. She laughed and did it again, this time curling her tongue around the bulbous tip. He tasted salty and musky.

She liked it.

Opening her mouth, she took him in. He was long and thick and she'd only done this once before, so she wasn't quite sure what to do. Following her instincts, she took him as deep as she could and then slid back to the tip, dragging her tongue over the sides as she did so.

Logan groaned and flexed his hips. "Your mouth is so hot. It feels so damn good."

Pleased, Kathryn quickened her pace. She jerked and Logan's cock popped out of her mouth when she felt something stroke her pussy. Gasping, she looked behind her. Marc's golden eyes were ablaze with an inner fire that she couldn't quite describe. Yes, there was lust but there was so much more.

"Don't stop." Logan tugged gently on her hair to bring her back to him.

Marc gave an almost imperceptible nod and Kathryn relaxed. She hadn't even realized she'd been tense, as if waiting for Marc to give his okay. Which was crazy, really. They weren't a couple or anything. They'd shared sex a few times but that was it.

Who was she kidding? Not herself. There was so much more between them than sex. They'd made love, or at least she had. Because there was no denying she loved Marc.

But right now, Logan was waiting. And she loved him too. Not in the same way as she did Marc but she needed to let him know how much she cared. How much she'd cared for years while he and Tienan had been all but prisoners to her father and the company.

She allowed Logan to pull her back to him. Putting all else aside, she focused her attention on pleasuring him. Wrapping her hand around the base of his shaft, she began to pump. Logan gave a moan of pleasure as she captured his cock head between her lips and began to suck and lick and stroke him with her tongue.

Behind her, Marc stroked her slick folds. She began to move her hips in tandem with his fingers. Cream slipped from her core as her need built. The taste and feel of Logan in her mouth and Marc's fingers teasing her pussy was an erotic combination that was overwhelming.

Logan's hips pumped harder and he drove his shaft deeper into her mouth with each thrust. She relaxed her throat, taking him as far as she could as she continued to squeeze and stroke the base. With her free hand, she gently cupped his testicles and rolled them between her fingers.

Marc slid one finger barely inside her opening, circling the rim. Kathryn moaned, the vibration running up and down the length of Logan's shaft.

Logan gave a hoarse cry, his entire body stiffening. She could feel the tightening of his balls and the surge of semen rushing through his cock as he came. Hot, salty liquid streamed into her mouth and down her throat. She coughed once, almost choking but she managed to swallow.

Marc thrust two fingers deep and Kathryn came undone. Crying out, she came as Marc stroked in and out of her core. Cream gushed from her pussy, dampening his hand as he continued to pleasure her. Her vision dimmed and she blinked. Marc's touch changed, becoming lighter, calming her as she tried to catch her breath.

Logan's hands remained fisted in her hair, his breathing harsh and ragged as he pumped his hips several more times. She tightened her fingers automatically, wanting him to gain the most pleasure possible. Slowly, he untangled his fingers and stroked her hair back over her shoulder. "Thank you."

She could sense the sadness in him and she knew that he understood that this was the last time they'd ever be together like this. When they returned home, things would be different. They'd be fighting for their very lives and there would be no time for relationships. Besides, her heart would be with Marc.

Kathryn nodded, releasing him and shifting her attention to Tienan, who was still propped up against the post at the end of the bed. How he'd slept like that, she had no idea. She expected that his shoulder was causing him some discomfort but she knew he'd never admit it. If she said anything about it, he'd only tell her that he'd slept in worse conditions. And she believed him. She had no idea about all the kinds of *training* the General had put him and Logan through but she knew it had been brutal and cruel, designed to break them as much as train them.

He looked relaxed and content. It was the first time she'd seem him like that. Usually, he was guarded and in total control. Tienan stared at her for what seemed like forever. As uncertainty began to take hold, he opened his arms to her.

She crawled forward, falling against his chest. It wasn't as wide as Marc's but there was undeniable strength there. His lean build was deceptive. Tienan was more than capable of killing a man with his bare hands.

But when he touched her, he was nothing but gentle. Gripping her shoulders, he eased her back so that she sat on her haunches between his spread thighs. His fingers played lightly over her face before angling down her shoulders and across her collarbone. "So delicate, yet so strong," he murmured as his fingers flowed between her breasts.

He rested his hand on her tummy and then sifted his fingers through her pubic hair, touching the sensitive flesh beyond. "So wet and hot and ready." He met her gaze, his green eyes practically glowing. "Will you let me have you?" She knew what he wanted. Last night could be brushed aside as in the moment of passion. This morning was deliberate.

She sensed that Tienan needed this from her and she wanted to give it to him. "Yes."

Marc watched as Tienan lifted Kathryn easily and lowered her onto his waiting erection. He couldn't look away as Tienan's cock disappeared into Kathryn's hot, tight pussy. Jealousy clawed at him but he shoved it away. This was what had to be. He wanted Kathryn to be sure when she chose.

But it was hard to watch his woman pleasure two other men.

Yet, there was a difference this morning. Sadness. Almost a finality, as if they all knew that this would never happen again. Marc felt it too. All his life he'd been a warrior. He'd faced death many times but this—this scared him to his very core. It felt almost as if Kathryn were saying goodbye to all of them.

Her hair flowed down her back, ending just above her heart-shaped ass. Tienan's face was buried between her breasts as he licked and sucked the tip of one and then the other.

Kathryn's moan of pleasure swirled around him, pushing him over the edge.

Marc had to touch her.

Coming up on his knees, he moved into position behind her. He didn't touch her, though. Not yet. As if sensing his presence, Tienan raised his head and glared at Marc before giving a sharp nod.

Marc placed his hands low on Kathryn's hips and pressed his erection against her supple spine. The heat of her body flooded through his cock and his balls drew up tight. Tienan positioned his grip above Marc's and began to lift and lower Kathryn. Marc caught the rhythm and together the two men began to move her up and down.

Kathryn's head fell back on Marc's shoulder and he turned her head, capturing her lips. He kissed her long and hard, all but devouring her as Tienan continued to fuck her hard. Shifting his hands from her hips, Marc cupped her breasts high and offered them to the other man. He felt Tienan's mouth brush Kathryn's tight nipples, licking, sucking and tugging gently on them.

Marc's cock was one huge ache as he pressed it against Kathryn's back. He knew that he wouldn't be able to hold out this time, knew he would spill his seed. But he didn't care. Tienan might be the one inside the tight clasp of her pussy but Marc was the one kissing her soft lips.

She tore her mouth from his and screamed. Marc could feel the orgasm take her. She stiffened and then her body began to quiver. Tienan thrust several more times and then yelled Kathryn's name. Marc wrapped one arm around her waist as he felt his own need rising. Burying his face in the curve of her neck, he gave a muffled cry as he came all over her back. He pumped his hips, pressing his cock as tightly to her as he could.

When he was done, he slumped back, their bodies making a sucking sound as they parted. Kathryn laughed and then groaned.

Tienan lifted her off his softening erection and she slumped against him. "I'm a mess," she grumbled. All three men laughed. Kathryn raised her head and glared at all three. "I want a bath and some food."

Logan reached over and ruffled her hair. "I heard someone in the bathing chamber a few minutes ago. I imagine there's a fresh tub of water."

"Oh great." Kathryn buried her face in her hands. "Now everyone will know what we were doing."

Marc rolled off the mattress and reached over to tug Kathryn out of bed. "They already knew." He held her hand until he was certain she was steady on her feet.

"That's just great." Taking several steps away, she propped her hands on her hips and glared at all of them but he could see the glint of humor in her eyes. "I'm taking a bath." She paused for emphasis. "Alone. Then I'll need some food."

Concern began to nag at Marc. They'd worked her body hard last night and again this morning. Plus, she hadn't eaten last night. He wasn't taking very good care of her.

"Hey." While he'd been castigating himself, Kathryn had come up beside him. "I know what you're thinking and you can stop it right now."

"And what am I thinking?" He was surprised by the fervor in her voice.

"You're thinking that maybe I pushed myself to much physically and that I need taking care of." He cocked an eyebrow at her but didn't deny it. She nodded decisively. "I knew it."

She poked her head around him so that she could see Tienan and Logan. "Tell him I can take care of myself."

"She needs a keeper," Tienan growled.

Logan rubbed his hand over his chin as if in thought but Marc could see the barely suppressed laughter on the other man's face.

"Men," Kathryn muttered, whirling around and stomping away. "I'm having a bath. I'll eat when I'm ready." They all watched as she strode off to the bathing chamber, completely unconcerned by her nudity.

As soon as she disappeared from sight, Marc turned to the other men. "I will take care of her." It was a pledge and a promise. Tienan and Logan stared at him as if testing the depth of his word. He met their gazes unflinchingly.

"We need to talk." Logan rolled from the bed and stretched.

Grabbing up his pants, Marc shoved them on. "We can bathe and talk down in the guest room. I expect Kathryn will be a while."

The three men left the room, each of them casting a glance toward the door of the bathing chamber and the sound of water splashing.

Chapter Twelve

𝕾

Scrubbed clean from head to toe, Kathryn felt better than she had in months, though her muscles ached and she had twinges in some strange parts of her body. *All the unusual activity*, she surmised as she walked down the stairs.

Thankfully, some kind soul had left her a clean pair of pants and a tunic, as well as a pair of short leather boots, so she hadn't had to put on yesterday's soiled clothing. She wasn't wearing any underwear though. Both her bra and panties had been in need of washing, so she'd cleaned them as best as she could in her bath water and left them hanging to dry. It felt odd to be bare beneath her clothing.

She'd been sorely tempted to stay in her room but this was her last day here. If she didn't look around the castle today she'd lose her chance and she so wanted to see everything. She was nothing if not curious.

Her booted feet made hardly any sound as she went down the stone stairs. She rubbed her hand along the wall, marveling at the building techniques. The castle was very well made. When she reached the bottom, she steeled herself before poking her head around the corner. The large room was almost empty. Many of the tables from the day before were gone and only a few remained.

Mara was busy at the head table but raised her gaze and glanced toward the doorway. "Come in, child. You must be hungry."

Kathryn went forward, purpose in every step she took. "I could manage a bite." In truth, she was famished for the first time in recent memory.

Laughing, Mara shooed her into a chair. "I'll get you something."

"You don't have to wait on me." She felt uncomfortable letting the older woman do for her when she was quite capable of getting her own breakfast.

"Of course I don't have to." Mara patted her shoulder. "But you've been through a few stressful days. Let someone else take care of you for a change."

Mara disappeared down a short hallway before she could protest. Relaxing in her chair, she looked around the room. A huge fireplace dominated the center of one wall. It was so big that several people could stand upright inside. The walls were all made of thick stone but the room was fairly well lit from windows near the top of the ten-foot walls. Most of the windows were made of plain glass but there were several with colored glass. The sunlight shot through the stained glass windows, creating cheerful patterns on the walls.

Above the fireplace several large swords were crossed and mounted, the jewels in their handles glinting. The wall opposite the fireplace was filled with a variety of very large tapestries, some of them at least four feet tall and even wider. The scenes on them varied from battles to daily life. All in all, it had a homey feel for a room so large.

Mara bustled back into the great hall carrying a tray with a steaming hot bowl of something that resembled oatmeal, some brown bread, thick slices of white cheese, a small bowl of berries and an apple. "I wasn't sure what you'd like, so I brought a bit of everything."

"You certainly did." Kathryn inhaled as the food was placed in front of her. The mouthwatering smells of fresh bread and honey made her stomach growl. Wasting no time, she dug into the bowl of hot cereal. It tasted nutty and was flavored with honey and, if she wasn't mistaken, cinnamon. "Delicious," she told Mara between mouthfuls.

"Good." Mara settled in the seat beside Kathryn.

"Where is everyone?" She barely stifled a groan of pleasure as she added a handful of the tart red berries to the bowl and helped herself to another mouthful. She couldn't remember when food had ever tasted so good.

"Jarek is out at the stables and Christina is still upstairs with the children."

Kathryn rested her spoon in the empty bowl and exhaled. She was pleasantly full but she still had room for a piece of the fresh brown bread. Maybe with a slice of the cheese. Helping herself, she bit into it and the flavor exploded in her mouth. She chewed and swallowed and then had another bite.

"Everyone else packed up and went home," Mara continued. "After what happened yesterday, no one wanted to tempt the ire of the sorceress." She paused, tapping her fingers on the arm of the chair. "Or you."

That surprised Kathryn. In spite of what had occurred, she hadn't thought that the warriors would step back from the challenge. She guessed that she'd underestimated the power of the tapestry. Of course, she still couldn't quite believe that she'd seen what she'd seen either. It had been an incredibly powerful moment.

She studied the woman sitting patiently beside her. She wore an ankle-length dress made of a sturdy fabric that had been dyed a flattering green. The bodice was embroidered with threads of different colors, their pattern a profusion of flowers. A belt that matched cinched the waist. Mara's long gray-black hair was coiled on top of her head and her blue eyes twinkled with a combination of warmth and humor. But there was both wisdom and compassion in those eyes. Kathryn looked away, suddenly uncomfortable beneath Mara's knowing gaze.

"I know this has been difficult for you," Mara began.

"Yes, it has been." Merely thinking about everything that had happened in the past few days was enough to make her breakfast churn in her belly. She took a deep breath and turned her thoughts away from it. She wanted to concentrate on the here and now, not on the past or the future.

"But the tapestry has brought you here for a reason. You are one of the few women who could thrive here. One who could make a difference."

"What do you mean?" Kathryn was curious to get the other woman's perspective.

"She means that with your skills and training you could benefit people from all around and not just those in this castle." Christina had come up beside them while they'd been talking. She was dressed similarly to Mara, in a dress dyed a deep, earthy-brown, her long blonde hair captured in a thick braid that hung to her behind. "And that's not to mention the fact that you're a descendant of the sorceress who crafted the magical tapestry and you have the knowledge to bring it forth."

"Yeah, well, that was pure luck." She felt the need to tell these women the truth. "When I did what I did yesterday, I had no idea if it would work. I mean, the chant is only words, right? There really isn't any such thing as magic." Except yesterday there was. The more she thought about it, the more confused Kathryn was by everything.

"Sometimes you simply have to accept the fact that you can't explain everything." Christina leaned against the table, crossing her arms over her chest. "Some things are just meant to be."

"I'm a woman of science, not magic. I believe in what I can test and see." And the fact that she couldn't figure it all out was frustrating her.

"Then how do you explain Marc traveling to your side to save your life and the tapestry bringing you all here?" Christina's voice was sharp, her irritation clear.

"I don't know." Exasperation rang in her answer.

"Don't fret." Mara patted her arm. "Know that you are here for a reason. It is up to you to find it and decide if it is worth staying. In the meantime, why don't I show you my herb garden?" Pushing back from the table, she stood.

Kathryn took a deep, calming breath and allowed her attention to be diverted. "I'd love to see your garden. I have some questions about several of the plants that were in the salve you gave me to put on Tienan's wound."

"I thought you might." Mara started for the door. "Christina?"

"I'm coming." Christina pushed away from the table and followed them but she stopped when she came alongside Kathryn. "Please don't break his heart. Marc's already been through so much."

Jealousy, anger and pain all shot through Kathryn at the possessive tone in Christina's voice. Marc had slept with this woman. Granted, Christina was Jarek's wife and she and Marc hadn't slept together in a while but still it made Kathryn's gut burn. Marc was hers.

She shook her head to try to get that thought out of her brain. She had to go home. There was no place for her here. A sharp pain bit into her stomach and she rubbed it absently.

"I'm sorry." Christina's voice was softer, her tone apologetic instead of accusatory. "I didn't mean to make your stomach act up."

"It's not your fault. It's been like this for a while now." For some reason, she didn't want Christina feeling bad. In spite of it all, she liked the other woman, who was kind by nature.

Mara spoke up. "Come along. We can stop in the kitchen. I can make you a tea that will help settle your stomach."

Trotting behind, she followed Mara down to the kitchen where she quickly steeped some herbs in hot water, creating a tea. Wooden mug in hand, Kathryn sipped the tasty brew as Mara and Christina took her on a tour of the castle and its grounds, introducing her to everyone who crossed their path.

* * * * *

Marc hurried down the stairs, strapping on his sword belt as he went. He knew that Kathryn had eaten and was long gone as he made his way down to the great hall. His conversation with Tienan and Logan had taken longer than he'd anticipated. They'd had many questions they'd wanted answered and he'd found that he had many questions of his own, not only about their lives on Earth but Kathryn's life as well.

Both men had refused to tell him more than the basics, informing him that it was up to Kathryn to tell him the rest if she so chose. What they had told him was enough for him to know that her entire life had been a living hell.

He rubbed his sternum as he hurried across the hallway toward the kitchen. He planned to have a bite to eat and then go for a long ride. One of the servants had informed him that Kathryn, Christina and Mara were touring the grounds. As much as he wanted to be with her, he was glad she was talking with the other women and exploring his home. Maybe that would influence her decision to stay. Or maybe it wouldn't. Only time would tell and that was quickly slipping away.

His heart ached for the child she'd been—one whose father had pushed and berated her, always letting her know that she wasn't good enough. Tienan and Logan had known her for years but they'd known about her long before they'd met her. Seems that her father had liked to talk about her in front of others. According to both men, that had made most of the staff at work dislike her before they'd even met her.

Tienan, in his quiet, thoughtful way, had said that he'd known she'd had a kind heart from the beginning. It was obvious in the way she interacted with people. Kathryn had only become aloof after she'd been rebuffed and ignored by her coworkers. Once she'd started working with he and Logan, she'd soaked up the positive attention they'd given her.

"They were too stupid to appreciate what a treasure they had." Logan's angry words still rang in Marc's ears.

Well, he wasn't stupid by any means and he knew what a treasure Kathryn was. They all did. And they all agreed on one thing.

Kathryn must be kept safe at any cost.

Striding through the kitchen, he grabbed an apple, a hunk of bread and some cheese, eating most of it as he continued on to the stables. His horse, Destiny, was waiting impatiently in his stall, stamping his hooves on the straw-covered ground. "I know you didn't get a run yesterday." He offered the apple to the enormous warhorse as he ran his hand down the animal's side. "I'm going to miss you, boy." Destiny stamped once again and shook his head but he sidled closer and took the apple from Marc's palm.

"Going for a ride?"

Marc gave the horse a final pat before turning to face his brother. "I need to clear my head."

"Is there anything I can do?" Jarek stood, hands on his hips, looking as strong and formidable as ever. But Marc could see the concern in his brother's eyes.

"No. There is nothing. Kathryn will make her decision when the tapestry arrives."

"You think she is going back to her own time."

"Yes." Marc grabbed a blanket and threw it over the horse's back. "Especially after what transpired yesterday."

"Those damn idiots," Jarek began but he broke off and began pacing. "I sent the rest of them packing at daybreak."

"I figured that most of them would go but I expected to be facing the Dannon brothers at least and perhaps the Hunters."

"Abrah came to me and told me that he'd thought about what Kathryn had said and she was right. The tapestry brought the bride to wherever she was supposed to be. Plus, the way she looked at you, it was obvious to all except maybe a few blind fools that she would have no other."

Marc was surprised but pleased. "That is good. I didn't want any more blood shed over this. Kathryn would never stay if that came to pass."

"He also hinted that he wouldn't be averse to the idea of Kathryn getting the tapestry to work its magic again."

Marc laughed, shaking his head. That sounded like Abrah.

Jarek stopped pacing and turned on his heel to face Marc. "That is the conclusion that most of us drew. She is important and not just to us. She has skills. We all saw what she did for Tienan. The woman is a healer, plus she has untapped magical powers as well."

"She'll deny the magical powers." From everything Tienan had told him, Kathryn was a woman who believed in what she could see and prove. He grabbed his saddle and tossed it onto Destiny's back, tightening the strap around the horse's belly.

"Denied or not, they exist. Many of the men, besides Abrah, are hoping that she can somehow make the tapestry appear again, bringing another potential bride, perhaps two."

"She will not stay," Marc blurted. He finished saddling the horse and faced his brother. "And I am going with her if the tapestry will take me."

All the color drained from Jarek's face and he swayed. "No." Reaching out, he grabbed Marc by the shoulders and shook him. "No. I forbid it."

Marc laughed but there was no humor in it. "You cannot forbid me." He felt no anger at his brother, knew his reaction came from a place of love. "She is my life. Without her I am dead."

Jarek jerked him into a rough embrace. "How will I survive without you by my side?"

"You have Christina and the children." Marc swallowed the thick lump in his throat. "I will have nothing if I let her go."

Jarek released him and turned away. He tipped back his head, shutting his eyes tight. Marc watched as his brother composed himself. When he turned back, there was only the slightest sheen in his eyes but his face looked older and more haggard than it had only moments before. "So be it." Striding to another stall, he began to saddle his own horse.

"Where are you going?" Marc gathered Destiny's bridle and led him from his stall.

"With you." He quickly readied his mount. "If you are determined to go, I would share this one last ride with you, my brother."

Marc nodded and swiped his face against his shoulder, unashamed of his tears. "One final ride." Swinging up on his horse's back, he waited until Jarek had done the same. Side by side, they rode from the stables, through the courtyard and out the castle gates.

Chapter Thirteen

ை

Kathryn meandered toward the stables, her thoughts filled with all she'd seen this morning. The sun was high in the sky and her stomach was informing her that it would soon be time for lunch. The air was clean and unlike anything she'd ever experienced back home where it was stale and sterile at best. Here the rich smell of earth and grass filled her nostrils. The only sounds she heard were of people laughing and talking as they worked and animals going about the business of living. It was incredibly peaceful and, in some ways, healing.

The castle was incredible. It was more like a mini city where Jarek was CEO and Marc the VP of operations. She snickered. That meant that Christina and Mara were the trusty executive assistants who actually ran everything, all the while letting the men think that they were in control.

They were incredibly self-sufficient here. They grew their own herbs and vegetables, as well as harvesting wild mushrooms, greens and berries. They raised cattle, pigs, sheep and goats for meat and milk, as well as for their hides. The women produced vast amounts of cloth for clothing, spinning and weaving it all in their homes. The men were all warriors but they were also farmers. There were two blacksmiths and a barrel maker, along with several carpenters and masons. The list went on and on. Anything that needed doing, there was someone skilled who could do it.

The blacksmith, who was actually Mara's brother, had wanted to talk to her about her tweezers. He was trying to make something similar but slightly larger so that Mara would have a pair to use in her healing duties. She'd found herself sketching designs in the dirt for several medical instruments.

A gruff man by the name of Dumphries, he had been intrigued and excited by the challenge of creating them, especially when she promised him that he could have her tweezers.

She'd met quite a few people today, including Mara's family, which consisted of her husband, their four children and her husband's brother. At first, everyone they'd come across had been reticent but they'd quickly warmed up to her, chatting and inviting her to view whatever they were working on or asking her into their homes. Christina and Mara were a great source of information. What those two women didn't know about the people and workings of the castle wasn't worth knowing.

And Mara. Kathryn was in awe of the other woman's knowledge of plants and their medicinal properties. She'd studied botany but Mara knew things that you couldn't find in books. She had a feeling she could talk to the older woman for years and still not learn a fraction of what the she could teach her.

Christina was skilled at spinning and weaving and had learned to cook since she'd come to Castle Garen as a bride. It was obvious that everyone there adored her. That was another reason that Kathryn couldn't stay. It would be awkward with the two of them here, wouldn't it?

Yet, Christina had hinted more than once that it would be nice to be able to talk with another woman who understood what she'd gone through and where she'd come from. Jane visited but it wasn't as often as either of them would like.

Kathryn had told her what had become of Earth. Christina had been shocked but not overly surprised by many of the changes. It had been easy to talk to both Mara and Christina and she'd enjoyed herself in spite of the fact that she knew she was leaving.

As beautiful as the castle was, as much as she liked the people she'd met and as much as Marc held her heart, her place wasn't here. This was a place of magic. She was a woman of science. Plus, there was the fact that someone had to stop her father and General Caruthers in their mad bid to control the world and destroy those outside the Gate. Earth needed changes if all its people were to survive.

She'd left her companions in the kitchen and gone in search of Marc. Jarek had met her just inside the main entrance. He seemed older than he had yesterday, the lines on his face deeper. Concerned, she'd asked him if he was okay.

He'd stared at her as if trying to see inside her, to read her very thoughts and examine her soul. It hadn't been a pleasant experience. Then he'd shaken his head and offered her a smile, telling her all was well. She didn't believe him but she hadn't called him on it either. He'd told her that Marc was still down at the stables and then left her standing there.

His mood had left her unsettled but she shook it off as she slipped past the stable door. It was darker in here and it took a moment for her eyes to adjust. The smells were more pungent here, more earthy. The scent of horses, leather and hay permeated the very walls of the place. It wasn't an unpleasant smell, merely different from anything she'd ever experienced. She'd only seen horses in books until she'd come here and she longed to actually touch one.

She crept down the long aisle and found Marc in a large stall, brushing a gigantic black horse. His large sword was leaning against the wall of the stall, allowing him more freedom of movement around the animal.

Leaning against the door, she watched him, once again taken by the broad strength of his shoulders and arms and the gentleness of his touch as he groomed the animal. The rhythmic motion of the brush was hypnotic. She could almost feel the touch as if it were her body he stroked.

Her breasts grew heavy and her nipples puckered. This was crazy. After last night, she figured she'd be sated for weeks to come. But the simple sight of Marc brushing the silky hide of his horse had all her hormones on alert. Her skin felt sensitized and the slight breeze coming in through the door ruffled her hair and made her tingle all over. Between her thighs, she could feel the folds of her sex growing thick and damp.

A soft sigh escaped her lips and Marc whirled around to face her, sword in hand. He'd moved so quickly, she hadn't even seen him draw his weapon. He held the heavy blade in front of her, both of them frozen in time. Then Marc cursed and sheathed his weapon, propping it back against the wall within easy reach. "I was lost in thought and did not hear you. I feared that maybe one of our guests had returned to challenge for you."

"Is that likely?" Christina had told her that the challenge was over, that all the single men had accepted the fact that the tapestry had brought her to Castle Garen.

"No." He turned back to the large beast and resumed grooming him. Marc seemed to be in an unusual mood. Or maybe it was a normal one. She didn't really know him well enough to say. In spite of that fact, she could sense that he was tense and out of sorts and she felt certain that wasn't usual for him. Not quite sure what to say or how to handle things, she decided to ignore it for now. If he wanted to tell her what was on his mind, he would.

The horse whinnied and stamped its large hooves. The long tail swished to one side and it turned its head and pinned her with dark, liquid eyes. She'd never seen anything quite like it in her life.

Kathryn sidled over closer, wanting to get a better look at the horse. Up close, it was huge. Much larger than she'd expected. She reached out her hand and then pulled it back. What if it didn't like her? What if it decided to bite her? She eyed the animal's rather large face and jaw. There had to be a lot of teeth in there.

"Do you want to touch him?"

Muscles worked in Marc's jaw but she didn't sense that he was angry or upset with her. She shifted closer and watched as the muscles in his shoulders rippled. "Yes. I've never seen a real horse before."

"Never?"

She sensed his surprise and smiled. "No. I've seen pictures in books but this is the first opportunity I've ever had to actually see a real one."

Marc smiled at her then and all her concerns fell away. The sun streaming in through an open window surrounded him, making him appear like some guardian angel or a hero from an epic poem. His brown hair flowed to his waist, caressing his bare shoulders and biceps. The vest he wore was open, revealing the hard planes of his chest. She'd touched that chest, slept with her face snuggled against it, yet like the horse, he seemed almost too good to be real.

He captured her easily with his golden-brown gaze and she leaned closer to him. She simply wanted to be near him, wanted to touch him. God, how she would miss him when she was gone.

Resentment filled her at the thought of having to return to her home. Why had the tapestry shown her this glimpse of heaven when she had to go back and right the wrongs of her father? It wasn't fair. But then, she'd learned early in life that fair had nothing to do with anything. Fair only happened in stories and fairytales.

"Give me your hand." He didn't wait for her to comply but reached down and captured her fingers in his. Slowly, he raised her hand to his lips, kissing each knuckle in turn before lifting it and placing it against the horse's neck.

She could feel the heat and the silky coat of the horse beneath her fingers. "What's his name?"

Marc shifted so that he was standing behind her, his chest to her back. Horse and man surrounded her. "Destiny." He slid his hand down her arm, raising goose bumps on her flesh.

She tried to concentrate on the horse but it was almost impossible as Marc's hands slid down her back and around her sides. He dipped his fingers beneath the hem of her tunic and pushed upward. Her breath caught in her throat as she raised her free hand, resting it against the horse's back. Destiny stilled, his large black body not moving a muscle.

The fabric bunched as Marc's hands continued their upward journey. Cream slid from her core and she bit her lip to keep from crying out. She wanted Marc and her body was making no secret of that fact.

"Feel the strength of the horse's muscles beneath your palms," he whispered as the edge of his hands brushed the undersides of her breasts.

As if all her senses were heightened, Kathryn could feel the muscles beneath her palms bunching and relaxing. She licked her lips, desperately trying to pay attention to the conversation but it was difficult. If Marc raised his hands the slightest bit he would be cupping her breasts. Her nipples tightened in anticipation. "I feel it."

He circled his hands around her breasts, his thumbs outlining her areolas but not quite touching them. "So soft."

It was the most exquisite torture imaginable. Kathryn knew they were taking a chance. Anyone could walk into the stables and see them. Her tunic was pushed over her breasts and Marc's hands were cupped around them. But the fear of being caught only served to heighten her arousal.

She pushed her hips back against him, moaning when she felt the hard length of his arousal against her bottom. Marc groaned, burying his face in the curve of her neck as he thumbed her nipples.

The sensation shot straight between her thighs. She was hot and wet and more than ready for him to fuck her. "Marc," she panted as he tugged gently on the turgid peaks.

"Hmm…" he answered as he ground his cock into her bottom.

"Someone could come in and see us." The smell of horse and leather and man was thicker now but underlying it all was the musky scent of arousal. Hers.

Marc nipped at her neck and then soothed the slight wound with his tongue. Kathryn sucked in a breath as her body responded to the caress. The crotch of her pants was soaked with her cream.

"I want you, Kathryn. I want to pull your pants down your sleek thighs, spread your legs wide and fuck you until you scream with pleasure."

She couldn't think. His words echoed in her brain until nothing else existed. No one or nothing else mattered. Right here and now, all she wanted was the man who was giving her such pleasure. She wanted his hardness buried deep inside her, soothing the ache that he'd created. "Yes," she moaned as he plied her nipples with his thumbs and forefingers.

He stiffened and then groaned as he went to his knees behind her. The ties at her waist were swiftly loosened and his hands slipped inside. His fingers grazed her hipbones as he shoved the pants down her thighs at the same time. She lifted one foot and then the other, allowing him to pull away her clothing, leaving her naked from the waist down, except for her boots.

"Beautiful," he murmured. His lips grazed the back of her leg. She jerked and then gave a breathless laugh, which quickly turned into a moan as his fingers moved swiftly upward. "Part your legs."

She didn't even give it a second though. The horse shifted slightly and Marc snapped out a quick command. The horse stilled in front of her, its body supporting her as its master probed between her thighs.

"You're so wet." She could hear the pleasure and wonder in his voice. "And it's all for me."

"Yes." She wanted him to know how much she wanted him, how much she cared.

He tilted her hips back slightly and his fingers glided over her slick folds. "You taste sweeter than honey." As if to prove his point, he stroked his tongue over her, swirling around her opening before dipping inside.

Kathryn rested her face against the horse's back. The hair was slightly prickly against her cheek but it was warm and solid. Her lungs were working hard now as she struggled to breathe. Her blood was hot in her veins, surging through her body and pooling in her pussy.

She cried out when his tongue flicked her swollen clitoris. The small nub of nerves was alive with sensation as he did it again and again. He pressed two fingers deep into her. Her inner muscles rippled, grasping at him as he withdrew and thrust again.

"Come for me, Kathryn. Give me your pleasure." His voice was ragged with lust as he worked her core with his fingers and her clit with his thumb. When he stroked the dark cleft of his ass with his other hand she gasped. Using her own juices, he coated his finger and rimmed the puckered opening of her behind before pushing inward.

The sensation was foreign but it was arousing. She could feel his thick finger where no one had ever touched her before. "Marc," she panted, not quite sure if she wanted him to stop or continue.

He took the decision away from her, pressing his finger farther into her ass. Her breasts swayed as she moved with him, wanting him deeper and harder. He continued to fuck her pussy with his other hand. Pressure built within her until it couldn't be contained any longer.

Orgasm hit her hard. Her legs trembled as she came. Cream slid from her slit, coating his hand with each contraction. "That's it," he encouraged. "Give it all to me."

Gripping the horse, she rode out the waves of pleasure, moaning in disappointment when Marc carefully withdrew his fingers from her ass and pussy. Before she could give voice to her frustration she was spun around.

Marc's eyes blazed with a combination of longing and lust as he cupped her ass in his hands and lifted her. Her legs twined around his waist automatically and she tilted her hips, rubbing against his thick length.

Her back was shoved up against the thick plank wall at the back of the stall. The fabric bunched around her shoulders cushioned her slightly. Marc leaned into her, holding her with the weight of his chest as he unlaced his pants.

"Hurry." She buried her hands in his hair.

He stopped long enough to plaster his lips against hers in a desperate, breath-stealing kiss. His tongue claimed hers and his mouth stole the very air from her lungs. Breathless, she kissed him back so hard their teeth clinked together. Her hands fisted in his hair as she held him to her.

How could she leave him?

The thought intruded, threatening to steal her pleasure. Then it was gone. Shoved away by the feel of Marc's hard flesh against her slick, tender folds. He positioned his cock at her opening and thrust hard, pushing every last solid inch inside her.

The horse nickered softly behind them but no other sound intruded. There was only the two of them, joined together, their breath mingling as they gasped for air.

She cried out as her body adjusted. Pleasure and pain warred briefly but pleasure easily won out. Gripping his shoulders, she hung on as he lifted her slightly. His fingers curved around her ass, holding her tightly as he sucked one taut nipple into his mouth and then the other. Back and forth he went, giving each puckered nub equal attention.

It wasn't enough.

"I need you to move." She tried to lift and then let her body fall back on his shaft. She only moved about an inch but even that sent tendrils of pleasure rippling through her. When he paused, she tugged on his hair, bringing his face up to hers. "Fuck me!" she demanded.

He growled low in his chest, his face almost feral in the dim light. But she wasn't afraid. She wanted him to lose control. She wanted him to take her hard and quick.

All thoughts about what was to come faded. Kathryn no longer cared if anyone walked in and found them. She didn't care that they were in a horse's stall in a stable. Nothing mattered but the physical and emotional connection between her and Marc.

Hitching her legs over his arms, he began to fuck her. Hard. His hips pumped faster and faster. She felt impaled by his thick length with every thrust. All her being focused on the heat building deep within her. Her thighs quivered and her hands clung to his neck and shoulders. His chest brushed her turgid nipples with every stroke of his cock.

Both of them were straining now. Reaching for it.

"Kathryn!" He cried her name as he rammed into her. His desperation was hers and she clutched him tighter, working her hips in rhythm with his thrusts.

"Marc!" She screamed as her entire being exploded. Stars danced before her eyes and her vision dimmed. Her body jerked, her hips grinding against his as a wave of heat filled her. She felt his cock swell inside her just before the flood of his hot essence filled her. She held on tight, wanting to feel every second, every sensation.

When it finally subsided, her head fell limp to one side and a bead of sweat rolled down her temple and into her eye. She blinked as it began to sting. Her hands slid from his slick shoulders and she hung there in his grasp.

Her senses gradually returned, making her very aware of the sights and sounds around her. The plank was hard against her back, her tunic a tight band around her upper chest. She was covered in sweat and her thighs were wet and sticky. When she shifted she felt a trickle of cream in the cleft of her behind, a reminder of what Marc had done. She'd found it incredibly arousing when he'd touched her there, pressing his finger past the tight opening of her ass.

The smell of sex surrounded them, hot and pungent. It mingled with the aroma of man, woman, horse, straw and leather. Kathryn knew she'd never forget it as long as she lived and that it would haunt her dreams for years to come.

Shifting her head slightly, she saw the horse in the far corner of the stall. The beast was watching them with its dark, soulful eyes. She shivered as a light breeze wafted over her, reminding her of their precarious position.

Marc raised his head and stared at her, his lips parting as if he wanted to speak. The horse whinnied and shuffled. Marc swore and slowly withdrew from her. Now that he was only partially erect, it was easy, yet her inner muscles grasped and clutched at him, trying to keep him within her.

The muscles in her thighs protested as she straightened. She was grateful for the wall behind her because she didn't think she could stand on her own. Her legs were like jelly.

She heard the voices then and they were getting closer. The fear of discovery propelled her away from the wall. Marc had already laced the front of his pants and run his hand through his hair. He looked the same as always except for the satisfied gleam in his eyes.

Thoroughly disgruntled, she frowned at him as she searched for her pants. Spying them, she bent down and grabbed them, barely stifling a shriek when he patted her on the behind. She shot him a dirty look as she shoved her feet into the openings and tugged her pants over her legs.

Whipping her tunic down, she finger-combed her hair as best she could, though she knew it was a useless endeavor. Anyone with a grain of sense would know what they had just done. Kathryn was sure she looked as if she'd just been tumbled in a stable.

What was done, was done. And besides, she wasn't ashamed of what had just happened. It was just awkward. She didn't want to meet someone she knew, having them speculate on what she and Marc had been doing.

As if sensing her unease, he smiled at her, stroking her hair from her face. "Thank you."

"You're welcome." She glanced at the open door of the stall. The voices were almost upon them.

"Wait until the coast is clear and then head back to the castle. You could use another bath." He plucked a strand of straw from her hair. She had no idea where it had come from. Before she could agree or disagree, he planted a rough, quick kiss on her mouth and was gone. He strode from the stall, pausing long enough to grab his sword.

She stood there, her fingers touching her lips. She could feel the heat of his mouth on hers and it sent a sweet pulsing to her core. "Stop it," she muttered under her breath. That's what had gotten her in trouble in the first place.

The men hailed Marc and she heard the low rumble of his voice returning their greeting. Creeping over to the door, she sneaked a quick peek. Two of the men she'd met yesterday — the head of the castle guard and the stable master — were talking with Marc. As she watched, he nodded and motioned to something outside.

When they finally began to move off, she heaved a sigh of relief. Something hit her shoulder and she whirled around. Destiny was right beside her, poking his large head out of the stall. "They're gone, which means I have to go to." Unable to resist, she stroked the horse's head one more time. Sighing, she patted his side and slipped from the stall, closing the door behind her.

The men were barely beyond the doors of the stable but their backs were to her. Swiftly and silently, she headed toward the castle door. All she wanted to do was make it back to her room without running into anyone.

When she finally made it into the cooler, darker depths of the castle, she sighed with relief. She could hear voices in the great room but figured she could slip up the stairs unseen. It would be close. As she passed the opening to the room, she glanced inside. Jarek and Christina were talking with Tienan and Logan. As if sensing her presence, Tienan looked right at her, his sharp green-eyed gaze missing nothing of her disheveled state.

Kathryn shivered. Wrapping her arms around herself, she hurried up the stairs, not stopping until she closed the door of her room behind her.

Chapter Fourteen

ෝ

Marc was still reeling from his sensual encounter with Kathryn in the stables. He could still taste her sweet essence on his tongue, still feel her heat wrapped snuggly around his cock as he thrust into her.

With a muttered curse, he brought his attention back to the men beside him, ignoring their startled gazes. He'd sensed Kathryn hurrying from the stables and while he understood her reticence at being caught making love in the stables, he resented it all the same. He wanted everyone to know she belonged to him.

One thing was certain, she would never forget the first time she saw a horse.

He chatted a bit longer and then headed to the castle. His long legs ate up the distance, his boots raising puffs of dust as he went. His first instinct was to seek out Kathryn but he knew she would want some time to compose herself. Besides, he would have forever with her. Right now, he needed to spend time with his family. As of tonight, they would be lost to him.

He swallowed hard at the thought of never seeing Jarek, Christina and his nephews again. Then there was Mara, his friends and all the men and women who were part of his daily life. For the first time, he understood the sacrifice that the tapestry brides made when they chose to remain in Javara. He admired their tremendous courage. To leave behind all that you knew and face the unknown was indeed a challenge. But it was worth it for love.

Tienan and Logan were seated in the hall along with his family. His nephews, Baron and Derrik played quietly on the floor beside their father's chair, their wide eyes never leaving the men. Marc felt a pain in the region of his chest and rubbed it absently. He would miss them all more than they would ever know.

He straightened his shoulders and strode forward, determined to spend the rest of the afternoon soaking up every single moment with them and storing it away in his memory for the years to come. Only for Kathryn would he leave them behind. They would miss him but they would be fine without them. Kathryn, on the other hand, needed him. And he needed her.

Acting as normal as possible, he joined the conversation. Jarek gave him a searching stare but Marc gave a small shake of his head. His brother bowed his head briefly before turning back to Logan. Christina gave him a quizzical look but he merely offered her a smile and a shrug. Then Mara called out to her, informing her that the baby was awake and demanding to be fed. She excused herself from the group and hurried off to feed her daughter.

Marc watched her leave, glad that she was here for Jarek to help ease the pain that his leaving would cause. He and his brother had always been close. A tug on his pant leg interrupted his dark thoughts. Baron leaned into his leg, watching him.

"Uncle Marc, what's wrong?" The boy had always been sensitive to the moods of others and saw way more than a child his age usually did.

Marc crouched down beside his nephew, who was really his son, and ruffled the boy's hair. "There is nothing wrong. I have a lot on my mind." Pain filled him at the thought of never seeing the boy grow into manhood, never seeing him swing a sword or ride a horse on his own. Baron had just begun to ride a pony and had taken to it with a natural ability. Marc's chest had almost burst with pride the first time he'd watched the boy trot around the courtyard on his own.

He would also miss watching the other children grow and change and he would never see any other children Jarek and Christina might have.

"It's about the woman, isn't it?" the boy persisted.

"Aye, it is." He patted the child on the shoulder as he stood. "But there is nothing for you to worry about." Taking him at his word, Baron went back to play with his younger brother. Marc leaned against the wall and watched them in their innocent play until he became aware of Tienan's presence beside him.

"They are beautiful children," Tienan remarked.

"They are."

"The eldest is your son." It wasn't a question. Marc inwardly cursed the fact that both the strangers from Earth were blessed with a keen intellect and eye.

"He is of my body but he is my nephew. Jarek is his father."

Tienan crossed his arms, his legs spread wide. There was nothing relaxed about his posture. "That must be…difficult."

"It is, but it is our way." He turned to face the other man. "I know what I am leaving behind when Kathryn chooses to leave but he will be loved and cared for by his parents."

"She is not going back there," Tienan stated calmly under his breath.

Marc shook his head. "I would prefer she stay but she is determined to go back. She feels responsible for her father's actions, for what happened to you and Logan."

"That is ridiculous," he insisted, voice even but green eyes snapping in anger.

"That is fact." Sighing, Marc pushed away from the wall and shoved a hand through his hair. "Do you not think that I wish she was less courageous, that she didn't feel as much responsibility as she does?" Dropping his hand back down by his side, he faced Tienan, understanding the other man's frustration. "But if she did, she would not be Kathryn."

Tienan swore. "It is not her place. Not her fight."

"You don't have to return either. You could stay."

A look of pure longing came over Tienan's face but disappeared almost immediately behind a mask of indifference. "That is my world and those are my people. I have heard rumors that not all the other alphas were terminated, that some of them actually made it out alive. I have to find them. Together, maybe we can fight the government and find justice for those outside the Gate."

He swiveled his head, his gaze pinned on the stairs as Christina descended with Kathryn by her side. "Besides, she is your woman."

Marc started to protest but Tienan's hand slashed through the air, stopping him. "Logan and I both know it. Yes, she cares for us but it is not the same. She loves you." His eyes narrowed. "And if you hurt her, I will find a way to travel through time and come back here and cut your heart out."

"She will not stay," Marc insisted. He'd seen the determination in her, seen her resolve to return.

"We will see." Tienan strode across the hall to greet them. Marc watched Kathryn's eyes light up with pleasure as the other man took her hand, leaned down and brushed a kiss on her cheek. From his vantage point, he could see the light blush creep up her face as she laughed and joined the group.

The afternoon was pleasant enough but everyone's mood deteriorated as time ticked by. The castle guard trickled in to sit at the long trestle tables that the servants had assembled but even their conversation was kept to a minimum.

By the time the evening meal was served, they were a quiet, morose group. Everyone knew what was coming, what the night would bring. The tapestry would appear and choices would have to be made. No one knew for certain what the outcome would be.

Mara had herded the children upstairs to their room after they'd said goodnight to all the adults. Marc had held each boy overly long, hugging them tightly, knowing that this was goodbye.

Jarek sat in silence, his actions getting tenser by the moment. Christina said nothing, sitting quietly beside her husband. Kathryn picked at her food, not eating much at all.

"Does your stomach bother you?" Marc hadn't thought to check with her to see if the food was acceptable. There was a thick beef stew, fresh bread, baked chicken and vegetables, as well as platters of cheese and fruit.

"It's all delicious, I'm just not hungry." She sipped the tea that Mara had placed in front of her. Marc wished he'd thought to thank the older woman for her thoughtfulness. She'd been taking care of the occupants of the castle for so long that all of them, including Mara herself, took it for granted.

"Try to eat a little bit more." She was still far too thin for his liking. Kathryn projected a confident, controlled facade to the world but physically she was delicate to the point of being fragile. He knew it was because of all she'd been through in her lifetime but especially the past few months. He only wished there had been time enough for her to get healthy before they returned. The past few days had only added to the problem, pushing her even further toward her physical limits.

She took two more spoonfuls of the soup before pushing the bowl aside.

It wasn't enough but time had run out.

Marc pushed his chair back from the table, ignoring the food still piled on his plate. "It is time."

Tienan and Logan stood, their expressions grave as they thanked Jarek and Christina for their hospitality. Christina started to stand but her husband put his large hand on her arm, stopping her. "They must do this alone."

Christina nodded but Marc saw the tears in her eyes as she hugged Kathryn. He knew she believed Kathryn was returning to her own time and that he would be left alone. His sister-in-law had no idea he planned to go with them.

He reached down and gave Christina a gentle squeeze. "All will be well. Jarek loves you and so do the children." She jerked her head back, her eyes searching his face. He could see the worry there and was sorry for it.

Jarek stood and, heedless of the audience watching them, yanked Marc into his embrace, hugging him tightly. Marc knew he had to get away before he disgraced himself with tears. He thumped his brother on the back, released him and turned away. Kathryn, Logan and Tienan were all waiting for him. He marched through the long hall with them at his side. He looked neither to the right nor to the left. And he never looked back.

He climbed the stairs for the very last time and led them to the room where they'd first appeared. Walking to the window, he stared out over the land for one final time, imprinting the picture on his heart and soul.

The door closed and he turned to face the group behind him. "I'm going with you."

Kathryn couldn't believe her ears. "What are you talking about?" Surely he didn't mean what she thought.

His eyes narrowed and he stared at her, resolve written on every line of his face. "I am returning to Earth with you when you go."

"That's ridiculous," she sputtered. "What's going on there is not your fight. Your life is here. Your family is here."

He strode to her, grabbed her shoulders in his big hands and shook her lightly. "Not my fight?" The tension from his hands radiated down her torso and legs until it enveloped her.

He was so much larger than her but she wasn't the slightest bit afraid of him. "No, it's not." There was no way she would let him leave his wonderful home and loving family. What he had here was everything she'd ever wanted. She bit her lip to keep from begging him to go with her. She loved him enough to want the best for him.

Marc lowered his face until their noses were almost touching, anger glowing in his eyes. "You are my life." He said each word slowly, spacing them apart. "You are the very air I breathe, the reason my heart beats. I will be by your side."

Her heart pounded so hard she feared it might explode from her chest. His words vibrated in her very soul. Never had anyone said such things to her. She'd wanted this kind of love her entire life, had longed for it, craved it. But now that it was being offered to her, she had to turn away from it.

"No. I won't let you do it."

He straightened slowly. "You cannot stop me."

Tears of anger and worry pricked her eyes and she swiped at them as she turned to the men standing silently behind her. "Talk to him. I'm going to get changed."

Stalking off, she headed to the bathing room, slamming the door behind her. Christina had told her earlier that her original clothing was all cleaned and waiting for her. Neither woman was sure if the clothing from Javara would make it through the transfer. Marc had arrived fully clothed but he wasn't from Earth and she wasn't about to take any chances.

Stripping off her pants and boots, she tossed them aside. She yanked the tunic over her head and added it to the pile. Had it only been two days since she'd been plucked from her bedroom and brought here? It seemed impossible, yet it had happened.

She tugged on her clean underwear and pulled on her pants, tugging up the zipper and doing up the single button. Her socks and shoes were next. She had no blouse, as that had been sacrificed as a bandage for Tienan. Christina had left a waist-length tunic for her to wear. It was better than nothing and hopefully she wouldn't lose it in the transition back home.

Even her purse was there, so she dug into the bag and pulled out her brush, then yanked it through her hair. When she was done, she quickly plaited the mass and tied the end off with an elastic from her bag. She tossed the brush back inside and looked around. There was nothing else left for her to do. She was ready.

She'd taken her tweezers downstairs earlier and given them to Mara, who would make sure her brother, the blacksmith, got them. Kathryn wished she'd be around to see how the man did with copying them and the other medical implements she'd drawn. Everything else she'd brought with her, including the leather journal, was tucked safely in her purse.

Taking a deep breath, she closed her eyes. There was no escaping her destiny, no matter what she wanted.

Are you certain you know what your destiny is?

The voice seemed to echo inside her brain, yet it wasn't hers. "Of course I'm certain? I have to go back." Great, now she was talking to herself. She had to get a grip.

Your destiny is not the same as Tienan's and Logan's. They have their path to walk and you have yours. Remember, child, the tapestry always knows what it is doing. It takes women who are out of place in their own time and brings them here, where they have the ability to thrive and make a difference.

The hairs on the back of her neck stood on end and goose bumps raced down her arms. She knew that voice. It was Sarainta, the sorceress. "I don't understand. It's logical for me to go back. This is not my time and place. Besides, I owe it to my people to go back and fight my father and the General." She turned in a circle, searching for the other woman. Her voice seemed to come from everywhere and nowhere in particular.

Sometimes you must push logic aside. Sometimes you must think with your heart.

"But logic is all I've ever known. It's how I've lived my entire life." Kathryn rubbed her hands over her arms, trying to drive back the chill that was slowly creeping through her.

Maybe it is time for your life to change. Maybe it is time for you to face your fears and claim your destiny.

"What fears? I'm trying to go back and face my father and General Caruthers. I'm trying to face my fears."

Are you really? The voice questioned kindly. *Or are you running from your biggest fear? The fear that you aren't really lovable, the fear that no one could truly love you for who you are.*

A lone tear seeped from the corner of her eye to trail down her face. "That's not fair," she whispered.

Life is seldom fair. But there are times when the scales can be balanced. This is one of those times. The choice is ultimately yours. Believe, Kathryn. Believe in yourself. The world you've known will get along, or not, without you. It doesn't need you. But this world…

A soft wind touched her face, drying her tear and then it was gone and she was left alone, Sarainta's final words left hanging in the air around her. Her thoughts tumbled over one another in her confusion. She had to go back. Didn't she? Was the voice right? Was she really running, out of fear, from her one chance at love?

The men all shouted her name at once and she raced back to the bedroom. She barely noticed that Tienan and Logan were dressed in their original clothing. Her attention was riveted on the bed. The tapestry sat on the end of the mattress, the threads glowing as the pattern swirled and changed.

The time had come.

Marc stalked to the bed and grabbed the tapestry. "I am going with you if the tapestry will take me." His voice was low and even.

She realized then that for him there was no other choice. He believed in love and was willing to do whatever it took for them to be together. He would sacrifice his home, his family and his friends to be with her, even knowing they were walking into certain death at the hands of her father and their government.

And what was she giving up? A chance to have a home and a family of her own. A place where she was accepted and her skills valued. A chance to spend the rest of her days beside a man who loved her more than life itself.

And what was she going back to? A world where she didn't belong. Where people belittled her and berated her. A lonely place with only two friends and no one to truly love her the way she needed them to.

"No." She whispered the word and Marc glared at her. She knew he'd misinterpreted what she meant.

Tienan strode to Marc's side and pulled the tapestry from his grip. "Logan and I are returning to fight." He turned to Kathryn. "There are rumors that some of the other alphas escaped termination. If that is so, we can start building an army, a resistance force outside the Gate to fight the government. Maybe band together with the people living there."

"Why didn't you tell me about that?" She was shocked that they'd kept this from her but pleased that some of the other men might have escaped.

"Because this is not your fight." His face was impassive as he looked at her. "Your presence would weaken us, give the General something to exploit."

Kathryn winced. His logic was irrefutable but it hurt nonetheless.

Logan came to her side and pulled her into his arms. "You are too good for that world of intrigue and ugliness. It is killing you. You belong here."

She wrapped her arms around him, hugging him tightly. "I don't want you to go. Not without me."

Logan kissed the top of her head. "We must go for now but perhaps this is not the end, perhaps we shall see each other again." He released her and she rushed to Tienan's side.

She flung herself at Tienan and he hugged her, the tapestry he gripped in his hands was warm against her back. "What about your shoulder?"

Tienan chuckled, although it sounded strained. "I am almost healed. Mara checked the wound and changed the bandage for me earlier."

"I should have done it," she whispered.

"No. You've done enough. Sacrificed enough. You have magic," he whispered in her ear. "You can bring the tapestry back to you and maybe someday we will return to visit you. It is best for all concerned if you remain here."

Tears coursed down her face unchecked as she turned to Marc. He waited patiently for her to make her decision. How could she pull him away from all that he'd known, all he loved and valued, to fight in a war that was not his?

The answer came to her in a blinding moment of clarity. She could not.

Her heart swelled in her chest as a love so huge it was almost too much to handle washed through her. She loved Marc with all her being. She loved him enough to leave her world behind, to send her friends back alone and to give up the fight against the forces of evil she'd left behind. She loved him enough to forego logic and to listen to her heart instead of her brain.

Deep in her soul, she wanted to stay. She was tired of fighting. Her entire life had been one long battle and she was weary of it. She'd done what she could by freeing Tienan and Logan to fight. Her part in that drama was done. The only thing she would do by returning would be to slow down both men in their battle for justice. And Tienan was right. She would be their Achilles heel, a weakness to be exploited by her father and The General.

It was all so clear now.

Logan went to stand beside Tienan, his hand on the tapestry so that it was gripped between the two of them. They both had swords strapped to their sides and daggers tucked into their boots. She prayed the weapons would make it back with them so they wouldn't be totally defenseless.

She almost snorted at her foolishness. Even without their swords and daggers, they were far from defenseless. Still, she worried for them and not just for their safety but for their mental and emotional well-being.

"I love you both." They nodded as one, neither of them speaking. But she could see the unspoken words in their eyes.

She turned to Marc and held out her hand. He took it in his much larger one, wrapping his fingers around hers and holding it securely. It would always be like that. Marc would always put himself between her and danger, keeping her safe.

Now she would do the same for him.

"I love you more than anything else in the world." She cupped his jaw with her free hand, loving the rough feel of the stubble against her palm. Marc was so vital, so alive.

"Are you ready to go home, my love?" He turned his face to kiss her palm as he wrapped his free arm around her waist.

"I'm already home," she whispered.

A brilliant light flashed through the room. Kathryn gasped, turning toward Logan and Tienan, desperate for one final glimpse of them. They both raised their hands in a silent salute.

Then they were gone.

Huge sobs erupted from her as she doubled over in pain. They were truly gone.

Marc pulled her into his arms, almost crushing her in his embrace. She let the tears flow freely then for the first time in her life. She cried for her painful childhood. She cried for the world she'd left behind. But mostly, she cried for the loss of the only two friends she'd ever known in her world.

"I don't understand," he said when her tears finally subsided. He released her, shoving her hair from her face, his actions almost rough. "Why didn't you go with them?"

She looked at his beloved face and offered him a smile. "Because you belong here and I belong with you."

The door to the bedroom banged against the wall as it was shoved open and Jarek burst inside. He gave a cry of gladness as he rushed toward them, pulling first his brother and then her into his arms. It took her a moment to make out his words. She froze as she realized that Jarek had known of Marc's intentions to leave with her.

"Thank you. Thank you. Thank you," he murmured over and over. All she could do was hug him back, knowing that Marc was by her side and she was standing where she was meant to be.

Chapter Fifteen

છ

Marc lay on his side, his elbow bent and his face propped on his palm. Kathryn slept beside him, her lips slightly parted. Every now and then she would emit a slight snore. He smiled at the soft sound.

The covers were tucked under her arms as she lay on her side facing him, her legs curled slightly. There were dark circles beneath her eyes but they would disappear once she started sleeping and eating on a regular basis. He planned to take very good care of Kathryn, coddling her until he felt she was back to peak health. These past days and weeks before he'd met her had obviously taken their toll.

He hadn't slept much last night, had been almost too afraid to shut his eyes, fearing that it all had been a dream. Instead, he'd been content to hold Kathryn in his arms through the dark hours of the night until the dawn.

The entire castle had been in an uproar last evening. Once they'd realized that Kathryn had stayed, a spontaneous celebration had broken out below in the great hall. The people were thrilled that another tapestry bride would live among them. Add to that the fact that Kathryn was a great healer with a touch of magic and they couldn't contain their joy. Their voices, raised in song and cheer, had rung through the stone castle for several hours.

But the joy had been tempered by the fact that Logan and Tienan were gone. Jarek and Christina had spent a short time with them before retiring below. Neither Marc nor Kathryn had joined the celebration. He knew that she was hurting at the loss of her friends.

Instead, he'd stripped her naked and tucked her into bed before removing his own clothing and crawling in beside her. He'd held her as she shed copious tears, each one a knife thrust to his heart.

Reaching out, he traced a long strand of reddish hair that fell over her creamy white shoulder and onto her collarbone. He ran his finger across the delicate bone, once again marveling at her resilience and strength. To give up all one had ever known for love was an amazing thing and he would spend the rest of his life making sure that she never regretted it. Her love was a gift he would cherish every day of his life.

"Hey." Her soft voice drifted over his skin like the lightest of touches.

He raised his gaze from her collarbone to her face. She blinked and smothered a yawn as she watched him. Her eyes were soft and warm, still filled with sleep. The cover shifted slightly, giving him a glimpse of a firm, white breast. His body tightened as his cock twitched to life. Last night had been about comfort. This morning, he wanted to claim her with his body. He wanted to pleasure her until she cried out her release.

Taking a calming breath, he slowly released it. There was time for that later. Right now she was awake and would need reassuring. "Good morning."

Sadness descended over her features as she sat up beside him, tugging the furs to cover her nakedness. "It really happened then. They're gone."

His gut clenched. Did she regret her choice? He didn't think he could bear it if she did. "Yes. They're gone."

She nodded, her green eyes luminous with unshed tears. She was so pale, her few freckles stood out on her heart-shaped face. Sighing, she rubbed her fingers over the thick fur on the bed. Marc's skin prickled as if it were his skin she stroked.

"Are you sorry I stayed?"

"Never!" He sat up beside her. "How can you even ask that?"

She shrugged and glanced away. Reaching out, he cupped her jaw, tipping her chin upward until she was looking at him again. "Don't ever be afraid to ask me anything, Kathryn." He caressed the side of her jaw with his thumb. Her skin was so soft and smooth. "You are my heart and that will never change, no matter how many years we both live."

She searched his face. He wasn't sure what she was seeking but she seemed to find it there. "I love you too."

Unable to bear the separation between them, he pulled her into his arms. Burying his face in her neck, he breathed in her essence. Her words seemed to heal a rift in his heart and soul that had been there for more years than he could remember. He was no longer alone. For as long as he lived, Kathryn would be by his side. His woman.

She flattened her hands on his chest, pushing him away. "Lie back."

He did as she asked, stretching out on the mattress with her seated above him. In the morning light, she resembled a nymph from legend with her long red hair twining around her body and her green eyes alight with pleasure. Her nipples peeked out from between strands of hair and he couldn't resist stroking them with his thumbs.

Moaning, she arched back, thrusting her breasts toward him. The motion brought the moist, damp folds of her sex down on his rock-hard cock. Marc rumbled with pleasure. If he shifted her the slightest bit, he could easily slide inside her waiting heat.

He wanted her to do it.

"Take me inside you. Claim me as your own," he urged, tugging gently on her nipples. Other than that, he remained motionless. He wanted her to do it.

Heat pulsed through Kathryn's body. It felt strange, yet right to wake up with Marc propped up in bed beside her, watching her. For a second, she'd wondered if it had all been a dream but reality had quickly descended. Tienan and Logan were gone and she might never know what became of them. She could only pray for their safety and hope that they found some peace and happiness in the world they'd chosen.

But she'd made her choice and she didn't regret it. Couldn't regret it. Not with Marc beside her. She was glad that the tapestry, along with the encouragement of her friends, had given her the courage to take what she wanted.

She believed Marc when he said she was his heart. She understood it too, because he was her heart as well. For the first time in her life, she truly knew what love was. It wasn't greedy or confining, it was giving and freeing. Marc would have given up his home and family for her. That meant everything.

His clever fingers tugged on her nipples, bringing a fresh surge of cream from between her thighs. Today was the first day of the rest of their lives and Kathryn wanted to celebrate being alive and being with Marc.

The hard length of his cock pressed against her and she shifted slightly, rubbing her clitoris against it. It felt so good she did it again.

Marc lay beneath her, solid and warm. "Take me inside you." He murmured. "Claim me as your own."

Hers.

He truly belonged to her as she belonged to him.

Raising her hips, she reached between her legs and wrapped her hand around his pulsing shaft. When he groaned, she pumped her hand up and down several times, licking her lips when liquid seeped from the tip.

"Kathryn." He said her name on a groan.

She no longer wanted to wait either, needing to feel him deep inside her body. Fitting the head of his cock to her opening, she slowly lowered herself. Her inner muscles stretched, encompassing his girth and length until he was all the way inside. Sitting on him, she wiggled slightly, wanting to make sure she had every last bit of him within her.

He clamped his hands around her hips, stilling her. "It will be over too soon if you keep that up."

Delighted, she laughed. She'd never thought of herself as a very sexual woman before she met Marc. He brought out another side of her. One she wanted to explore.

"Like that idea, do you?" he teased as he squeezed the globes of her ass. This time it was Kathryn who moaned. Then he ran his finger over the dark cleft of her behind, rimming the puckered opening.

"Yes. No." She no longer knew what they were even talking about. Her body and her soul were on fire for the man beneath her. The primitive need to claim him welled up within her, urging her to move.

Following her instincts, she raised up on her knees until only the wide head of his cock was still within. Then she sat down heavily, driving him deep. Her inner muscles rippled. It felt so good that she did it again and again.

Marc stroked over her slick folds as she rose, coating his fingers with her cream before returning to her behind. This time when he rimmed her ass, he pushed inward. The tight muscles protested slightly and then gave as his finger slid inside.

With his cock in her pussy and his finger in her ass, she felt surrounded by Marc. He let his finger slide, keeping time as she continued to lift and lower her sheath over his straining cock. She could feel him swelling inside her and knew he was close.

"Marc," she cried his name, not quite knowing what she wanted.

He withdrew his finger and pulled her down on top of him. Her breasts crushed against the hard planes of his chest as his mouth captured hers. Then he rolled, keeping them joined from mouth to pelvis.

He truly surrounded her now, his weight a delicious reminder of the differences in their sizes and strengths. Yet, they were equal when it came to the passion raging between them.

Releasing her lips, he left a trail of hot, wet kisses on his way to her breasts. He sucked one nipple and then the other, until she was almost mindless with pleasure. Release hovered just out of reach.

Planting her feet against the mattress, she pushed upward. Marc sat back on his heels, hooked his arms beneath her thighs, spread her legs wide and began to thrust. His hips pumped hard and fast.

There was nothing she could do but dig her hands into the covers beneath her and hang on as he took them both over the edge. They came at the same moment, an explosion of sensation. She cried out as her hips jerked. The hot flood of his semen filled her, lengthening her orgasm until it felt as if it would never stop. He tilted back his head, the cords of his neck straining as he came.

Eventually, his chin dropped forward onto his chest, his long hair obscuring his face. He lowered her legs and slid away from her. She couldn't bear the separation and tugged him down into her arms. He came readily, dropping onto the mattress beside her. Curling his arm around her, he pulled her into the curve of his shoulder.

"You're mine," she whispered as she toyed with a strand of his brown hair.

Slowly, he raised his face, his expression solemn. "I am...and you are mine." It was a pledge, a promise, that neither one of them would ever forsake.

"Destiny is a funny thing," she began, walking her fingers over his chest.

"It is," he agreed as he cupped her breast in his hand.

She stilled. "Again?" she gasped almost breathless at the thought.

"Again." He smiled as he lowered his mouth to hers, their lips touching in a tender caress.

* * * * *

It was several hours later before Kathryn thought about what she'd meant to say to Marc. They'd gotten sidetracked. She wrapped her arms around herself and laughed, just thinking about what they'd done. He couldn't seem to get enough of her.

Destiny was a funny thing. She'd found the tattered book in the attic. Inside its pages she'd first met Marc. Then she'd discovered the journal and the tapestry. All of it had led her here. She could almost here Sarainta's laughter echoing in her mind.

Our lives are bound. Connected with the finest of threads, which reach across time and space to touch and knit together to form something new.

"Threads of destiny," she whispered as she picked up her purse in search of her brush. Her hand struck something soft and square. Wrapping her fingers around it, she tugged out the journal, opening it to the final page she'd read. But there was now more writing scrawled across the paper.

Sitting down on the edge of the bed, she read her own story. She knew that the journal didn't pass judgment on the choices people made. That could only be done by the people who made them—for good or for bad.

She sighed and started to shut the book but something made her flip through the blank pages at the back. Writing jumped out and she stopped. The page was blank except for two names—Tienan and Logan.

Her heart began to pound. Maybe she would find out what happened to them. Someday. Her fingers traced over the empty page, willing more writing to appear but it remained unchanged.

Perhaps at some point in the future the tapestry would bring them back to Javara. But she didn't really believe that would happen. The tapestry's magic was in its ability to seek out women who could thrive here. She knew the secret of calling the tapestry but she had no idea how to make it bring her friends back to her. Even magic had logic and rules governing it. Maybe in time, she'd understand more.

The door to the room opened and Marc stepped inside. "Are you ready?"

Kathryn closed the journal and tucked it and her brush back into her purse. Her heart felt lighter. If their names were in there, she at least knew that they were still alive. That was something.

Rising, she shook out the folds of the pretty green dress that Christina had brought her. The bodice was embroidered with colorful flowers and the sleeves went all the way to her wrists. The fabric was fitted to the waist and then fell in soft folds all the way to her ankles. On her feet were soft, leather shoes. She normally didn't like dresses but today was different. Today she was marrying the man she loved.

"I'm ready." Walking over to Marc, she took his hand.

He raised her fingers to his lips and kissed it. "Together."

"Together," she echoed as they walked down the stairs to the crowd waiting below.

Also by N.J. Walters

∞

eBooks:

Amethyst Dreams

Amethyst Moon

Anastasia's Style

Awakening Desires 1: Katie's Art of Seduction

Awakening Desires 2: Erin's Fancy

Awakening Desires 3: Capturing Carly

Awakening Desires 4: Craving Candy

Awakening Desires 5: Jackson's Jewel

Beyond Shadows

Dalakis Passion 1: Harker's Journey

Dalakis Passion 2: Lucian's Delight

Dalakis Passion 3: Stefan's Salvation

Dalakis Passion 4: Eternal Brothers

Dalakis Passion 5: Endless Chase

Drakon's Treasure

Ellora's Cavemen: Dreams of the Oasis IV *(anthology)*

Ellora's Cavemen: Jewels of the Nile IV *(anthology)*

Ellora's Cavemen: Legendary Tails IV *(anthology)*

Ellora's Cavemen: Seasons of Seduction III *(anthology)*

Hearts of Fire 3: Seeking Charlotte

Hearts of Fire 5: Entwined Hearts *(with Ciana Stone, Nicole Austin, TJ Michaels)*

Jessamyn's Christmas Gift

Feral Fixation *(anthology)*
Overtime, Under Him *(anthology)*
Summersville Secrets 1 & 2: Summersville Heat
Tapestries 1 & 2: Tapestry Dreams
Tapestries 3: Woven Dreams
Three Swords, One Heart
White Hot Holidays Volume 3 *(anthology)*

About the Author

෨

N.J. Walters worked at a bookstore for several years and one day had the idea that she would like to quit her job, sell everything she owned, leave her hometown and write romance novels in a place where no one knew her. And she did. Two years later, she went back to the same bookstore and settled in for another seven years.

Although she was still fairly young, that was when the mid-life crisis set in. Happily married to the love of her life, with his encouragement (more like, "For God's sake, quit the job and just write!") she gave notice at her job on a Friday morning. On Sunday afternoon, she received a tentative acceptance for her first erotic romance novel, Annabelle Lee, and life would never be the same.

N.J. has always been a voracious reader of romance novels, and now she spends her days writing novels of her own. Vampires, dragons, time-travelers, seductive handymen and next-door neighbors with smoldering good looks all vie for her attention. And she doesn't mind a bit. It's a tough life, but someone's got to live it.

෨

The author welcomes comments from readers. You can find her website and email address on her author bio page at www.ellorascave.com.

Tell Us What You Think

We appreciate hearing reader opinions about our books. You can email us at Comments@EllorasCave.com.

Why an electronic book?

We live in the Information Age—an exciting time in the history of human civilization, in which technology rules supreme and continues to progress in leaps and bounds every minute of every day. For a multitude of reasons, more and more avid literary fans are opting to purchase e-books instead of paper books. The question from those not yet initiated into the world of electronic reading is simply: *Why?*

1. *Price.* An electronic title at Ellora's Cave Publishing runs anywhere from 40% to 75% less than the cover price of the exact same title in paperback format. Why? Basic mathematics and cost. It is less expensive to publish an e-book (no paper and printing, no warehousing and shipping) than it is to publish a paperback, so the savings are passed along to the consumer.

2. *Space.* Running out of room in your house for your books? That is one worry you will never have with electronic books. For a low one-time cost, you can purchase a handheld device specifically designed for e-reading. Many e-readers have large, convenient screens for viewing. Better yet, hundreds of titles can be stored within your new library—on a single microchip. There are a variety of e-readers from different manufacturers. You can also read e-books on your PC or laptop computer. (Please note that Ellora's Cave does not endorse any specific brands.

You can check our website at www.ellorascave.com for information we make available to new consumers.)

3. *Mobility.* Because your new e-library consists of only a microchip within a small, easily transportable e-reader, your entire cache of books can be taken with you wherever you go.

4. ***Personal Viewing Preferences.*** Are the words you are currently reading too small? Too large? Too... ANNOYING? Paperback books cannot be modified according to personal preferences, but e-books can.

5. ***Instant Gratification.*** Is it the middle of the night and all the bookstores near you are closed? Are you tired of waiting days, sometimes weeks, for bookstores to ship the novels you bought? Ellora's Cave Publishing sells instantaneous downloads twenty-four hours a day, seven days a week, every day of the year. Our webstore is never closed. Our e-book delivery system is 100% automated, meaning your order is filled as soon as you pay for it.

Those are a few of the top reasons why electronic books are replacing paperbacks for many avid readers.

As always, Ellora's Cave welcomes your questions and comments. We invite you to email us at Comments@ellorascave.com or write to us directly at Ellora's Cave Publishing Inc., 1056 Home Avenue, Akron, OH 44310-3502.

MAKE EACH DAY MORE *EXCITING* WITH OUR

ELLORA'S
CAVEMEN
CALENDAR

☥ WWW.ELLORASCAVE.COM ☥

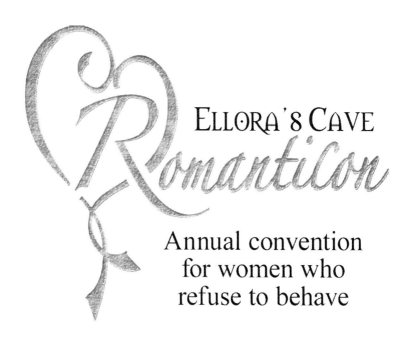

ELLORA'S CAVE
Romanticon

Annual convention
for women who
refuse to behave

CPSIA information can be obtained at www.ICGtesting.com
Printed in the USA
LVOW131708030213

318412LV00001B/287/P